AFTER NIGHTFALL
&
Other Weird Tales

AFTER NIGHTFALL
&
Other Weird Tales

David A. Riley
Illustrations by Jim Pitts

PARALLEL UNIVERSE PUBLICATIONS

ISBN: 978-1-9161109-6-0
Parallel Universe Publications, 130 Union Road,
Oswaldtwistle, Lancashire, BB5 3DR, UK

Thanks to my wife Linden
For her support & encouragement
And everyone who published these
stories to start with:
Trevor Kennedy
Jason V. Brock
James R. Beach
David A. Sutton
Stephen Jones
Graeme Hurry
Mike Davis
Joseph Rubas
Stuart David Schiff
&
the late Richard Davis
Plus
Jim Pitts
for creating such
marvellous illustrations

CONTENTS

INTRODUCTION

Over the years I have had three volumes of short stories and four novels published and have never written an introduction for any of them, but this collection is something different, and perhaps deserves a bit of an explanation, with its random selection of stories ranging from some of my earliest (1970) to one of my latest (2020).

So, what decided the stories in this collection and why?

Simply put it came about when I realised several months ago that quite a few of my tales had already been illustrated by my long-time friend, the fantasy artist Jim Pitts, starting with 'The Shade of Apollyon' and 'Terror on the Moors' in the short-lived high-street magazine *World of Horror* in 1974. This was followed a few years later by an illustration in *Fantasy Tales* for 'Writer's Cramp', for which, by a curious coincidence, Jim created an even more elaborate piece of artwork in 1994 for *Northern Chills*, a hardback and paperback anthology edited by Preston publisher Graeme Hurry.

The tipping point came when Trevor Kennedy asked Jim to illustrate my story 'The Fragile Mask on his Face' for *Phantasmagoria* magazine, which Trevor used in full colour for the front cover with a black and white version inside. Then, when Trevor went on to ask Jim to illustrate 'Three Eyed Jack' for his anthology series *Gruesome Grotesques*, the idea for this collection began to form.

Jim and I decided a further four stories were needed and chose 'Fish Eye', 'Boat Trip', 'Prickly' and 'After Nightfall'. And thus, as simply as that, this project was born.

It has been an enjoyable experience, perhaps because Jim is such an easy person to work with and produces some amazing artwork.

I hope you the reader enjoy the stories, both the old and new, with the truly remarkable illustrations that accompany them.

David A. Riley,
Oswaldtwistle, 2020

THREE EYED JACK

Jack was born with three eyes, which resulted in his father, Bert Houraghan, calling his mother, Patty, a whore because no son of his would be born a freak. That was the last she saw of him. He walked out, got drunk in his local pub and walked under a bus.

His mother took to drink as well, which became a lifelong occupation, in between trying to think of ways she could exploit her son's 'peculiarities'.

Jack had two normal eyes like everyone else, so pale blue in colour they were almost grey. In the exact centre of his forehead, though, was a third eye, slightly smaller than the others and an intriguingly vivid violet, which would have been appealing had it been a normal eye in the right place but disturbingly unsettling where it was.

For most of his youth Jack usually wore a bandage or a bandana to hide it from view, though of course it wasn't something that could be kept secret from his fellow pupils at school, some of whom might have been tempted to tease him about it, except luckily for Jack he was large and strong and intimidatingly aggressive. Few, therefore, were ever tempted to taunt him about it, and those who did soon regretted their mistake.

Which didn't make for a happy or an easy school life, which ended prematurely when Jack was expelled at age fourteen for persistent fighting. But by then his mother, who as usual was chronically short of money, had met up with Harold Pettifer, an entrepreneur of a dubious sort who specialised in the 'entertainment business'.

Although Freak Shows were no longer a legitimate form of entertainment even in travelling circuses, there were other ways in which Harold thought they could all make some money.

"Fact is that third eye is real. Everyone can see that," he told Jack and his mother in their cramped, untidy living room over several cans of beer and a coke for Jack, who was still only fifteen. "Which means we can convince people the boy can see beyond the Veil." He smiled, self-satisfied at the phrase, which he relished. A small man, he was well into his fifties, though he looked much older after years of booze, chain-smoking Havana cigars and a haphazard, sometimes hazardous life during which he had always somehow just about managed to keep a few inches ahead of the Law, not to mention numerous businessmen, actors, singers, theatre-owners and other entrepreneurs he had bamboozled with his schemes.

"But he *can* see things beyond the Veil," Jack's mother said. She lowered her voice into a whisper even though there were only the three of them there and they could hear perfectly well what she said: "It all happened when he started puberty."

"Mum!" Jack's face went red as if someone had slapped him on both cheeks.

Patty looked at him "There's nothing to be embarrassed about, son. It happens to us all."

"Too long ago for me to remember, alas," Harold said with a titter.

Patty humphed. "Of course, some of us were probably born old," she countered.

Harold tittered again then poured himself more beer. "Tell me," he said, "what Jack can see."

"He doesn't like to talk about it. It scares him sometimes. Which is why he prefers to keep that eye covered over so there's no chance of it accidentally opening, like, and him catching sight of something he don't want to see."

Harold gazed at Jack with added interest. "I thought we would be pretending he could see something."

14

Patty shook her head. "We still will. There's nothing he sees that'd be any use to you or me with this clairvoyance business. He doesn't see no Indian medicine men or things like that. Just *things*."

"Things?"

Jack squirmed. "You know I don't like to talk about them."

His mother patted him on his shoulder.

"That's all right, Jack, we won't. Harold here will tell us what we need to do instead. That's right isn't it?" she asked, turning to Harold.

"Of course, of course." Harold sipped some beer, then said, "Back in the day there was a clairvoyant I once acted for as his agent. Mystic Mike, he was called. He was quite big in Rochdale and Bacup. Filled the Theatre Royal once, well the stalls anyway. Would have gone on to better things but he got into trouble with the social and ended up doing six months."

"He didn't see that coming, did he?" Patty said with a giggle.

Harold shook his head. "The old one's are always the best, aren't they? Though I hate to point out he was a clairvoyant not a fortune teller."

"Still, what is it we're going to do with Jack? Are you going to teach him some tricks?"

Harold nodded. "With that mystic eye in his forehead he'd be a sure-fire winner. No one would doubt he could see things hidden from the rest of us with it."

Jack squirmed and muttered something that Harold couldn't quite make out.

"What was that, Jack?" he asked.

Patty said: "He can see things with it. That's what I was telling you before. They scare him."

Harold frowned. "Does that mean he won't open that

eye? That's the big gimmick. Without that none of this will work."

"That's up to him." Patty turned to Jack. "They're not there every time, are they, love?" she said. "If you just take a peep you're all right mostly, aren't you?"

Jack nodded, though he seemed less than happy.

"Well, I can teach him all the tricks," Harold said. "If Mystic Mike could learn them anyone can."

For the next few weeks Harold worked to get Jack as proficient as possible at *clairvoyancey*, as he termed it. It wasn't easy. Jack was a slow learner, which helped to explain some of his problems at school. It wasn't all because he had a third eye. But, after a month had gone by Harold told Jack's mother he thought the lad was ready.

"Or as ready as he'll ever be," he added with a slight sourness that drew a frown from Patty.

"He's a good lad," she said. "Just lacks a bit of perseverance."

"He'll need to use a bit of that when we get going." Harold tapped the table between them for emphasis. "For the most part we might only be dealing with some silly old biddies who want to believe they'll hear from their loved ones and are easily fooled, but there's always one who's a bit sharp. We'll keep it simple. Four or five at a session, no more to start with."

"Not the Theatre Royal?" Patty asked.

Harold laughed. "Mystic Mike was a showman. He could handle crowds. Audiences lapped up every word he said. I don't think Jack's quite up to that yet. Baby steps, eh? Just baby steps to start with. With that eye of his word will soon get around, never you mind. And by then let's hope Jack's mastered the trade."

In his mind Harold could already see the twenty-pound

notes piling up, stack after stack of them.

Jack was sweating. It beaded down his face as if he'd just had a shower. He didn't like taking the bandana off. He felt safe with it on, secure. He disliked opening that eye even more. It was months since he'd last taken a peek and he hadn't liked it. Even the look of awe on people's faces when they stared at it didn't make him feel any better. It was like being a freak. A weirdo. That was what that spotty fat pilluck Danny Bleasdale called him, before he split his lip and chipped one of his teeth with his fist. That got him suspended for a month, but it had been worth it.

There were five ladies waiting in the parlour, which Harold had carefully refurnished out of his own pocket to give it the right atmosphere, with a big round table in the middle and wooden dining chairs all around it, a chandelier hanging from a brand-new plaster rose in the ceiling. It gave off a brilliant light, which wasn't how Jack imagined seances were usually lit, but Harold said it was important that everyone could see his third eye. And that it was real.

For which he would have to open it.

He knew some of the things he might see, things people couldn't otherwise even imagine were there. He'd seen a man with a huge tick the size of a lilo hanging on his shoulders, sucking away at the back of his neck with a nasty hook-shaped beak. The man had walked with a bent back, and no wonder! He'd seen a woman with an amorphous great jellyfish smothering her head. She had blank-looking eyes and didn't seem to know where she was. Then another time he saw a man, a building-worker with a high-vis jacket and plastic helmet, cursing and swearing on his way home from work. He was surrounded by glowing, iridescent creatures that stung him repeatedly. Each time they did so he got angrier and angrier.

Jack hated seeing these things, knowing that so many people had parasites feeding off them, making them act weird. Some even grew inside people and only bits of them showed. These scared him the most.

He couldn't tell any of the people who came to him about these. They'd think he was mad or lying.

Better stick to what Harold had taught him to say.

"Well, here we are," Harold said as they gathered in the parlour. He was going to get it going then sit at the back of the room out of the way and let Jack get on with things. It was a trial run, and afterwards he and Jack would iron out any problems so next time things would go smoothly. Or that, at least, was the plan.

Harold had chosen the ladies who were present with care. Mrs Clement was a widow of thirty years, whose husband died of cancer when he was only forty-seven. She had missed him ever since and was a regular at seances like this, and as gullible as you could get, never once noticing inconsistences between what one clairvoyant told her and the next. Mrs Palmer was a different kettle of fish. She was only forty and her husband was still alive. It was her dear, devoted mother she was hankering after hearing from, dead this last six months. This was her first seance. A close friend of Mrs Clement, Harold thought she was probably just as easily pleased. There were two other friends, Mrs Hammett and Mrs Mains. Harold had told him everything he knew about them too, which was part of how they would be tricked. The more he knew about these people the easier it was to convince them he was in touch with their loved ones. The fifth was the hardest, Miss Darlington. Emily Darlington was a retired schoolteacher and spinster. She was tall and thin and coughed a lot. She had no close relatives and her parents were still alive, safely looked after in a nursing home. Harold wasn't sure who she was trying to contact, though she had lost a dog, a miniature poodle called Spike a few months ago. Surely not, Jack thought. But Harold had said just let on that the dog is all right and is missing her but happy in his new home. Jack frowned. That sounded soft and pathetic, but Harold did know what he was talking about. At least that's what the little man claimed.

Jack smirked, though he still felt queasy inside.

"Here we go," Harold said, interrupting his thoughts. "Showtime." One of Harold's favourite words which irritated Jack. At least it helped take his mind off his worries.

Jack was introduced to the ladies who shook hands with him, some more diffidently than others.

Harold explained a little about Jack, telling them that his 'unique insights' were due to having been blessed with a third eye, which drew gasps of astonishment from everyone apart from Miss Darlington, who frowned. Jack knew she would be the most astonished when he revealed the eye to her, and she saw it was real. That would blow away her scepticism with a vengeance!

They took their seats at the table, all of the ladies staring at Jack, which made him feel uncomfortable, especially as he was dressed in a suit Harold had only just bought for him. He was more used to track suit bottoms and a hoody; he felt as if he was trapped inside a straitjacket. Harold had also purchased a dark blue bandana for him to wear over his eye rather than the piratical one he normally wore. He missed that too. This smelt of starch and was stiff.

"Perhaps, Jack, you would remove that bandana and we could start," Harold said from his seat at the back of the room.

Jack wished he had a can of coke, his throat felt so dry. He was sure for one panicky moment he wouldn't be able to speak, let alone talk about what they wanted to hear. All the information Harold had drummed into him seemed to cascade through his head like so much confetti.

Jack reached up for the bandana and eased it off. The eye was closed. It had been closed for months. Gently, he rubbed it with one finger to clear the grit from its lashes. Then, holding his breath in anticipation of what he might see, he opened it and looked round the table.

"Oh, my goodness," one of the ladies whispered in awe. When the eye turned and gazed at her she fanned her face as if she were about to faint.

Jack breathed in deeply as Harold had told him to do to calm himself and give the impression of concentration.

He was relieved to see only the astonished faces of the women as they stared back at him apart from only one 'creature', a bright red snake that hung in coils about the neck of Miss Darlington, its mouth facing hers as it shared her breath. No wonder she looked so thin and was always coughing, Jack thought. That creature was stealing away her breath. Not that Jack knew how he could tell her or what they could do if he did. As if aware he had seen it the snake turned its head and looked at him. It had round eyes like amber marbles, one of which it shut in what Jack was sure was a knowing wink, which rattled him for a moment till he heard Harold cough from behind the ladies. Unlike Miss Darlington's cough, Harold's was peremptory. Then the lessons kicked in and Jack was surprised how easy it was. Before he knew it the hour they had been allotted was over and they were getting to their feet, chattering to each other in amazement.

Harold rose to see them out.

It was the first time Jack had seen the little man since the seance started. He was startled at what his third eye saw. Harold was surrounded by strange-looking creatures that hung from him like bald ferrets, their skin all wrinkly and purple, with dark blotches. They were evil-looking things that tried to scramble past each other to whisper in his ears. A kind of umbilical cord connected each of them to the man, disappearing inside his clothes.

Jack instinctively shut his eye, but it was too late. Knowing this he opened it again to see the creatures staring at him.

Gulping, Jack reached for his bandana and pulled it over his head till it covered the eye. He had had enough for one day.

And more than enough of Harold.

"Are you all right, lad?" the little man asked.

Jack grunted something, repelled by him but unwilling to say what he'd seen. Even without the eye open he could sense the creatures hanging from him and he wanted to keep away from them.

Luckily, his mother came into the room.

"Well, how did it go?" she asked, her speech slurred from spending the afternoon in the Bell and Compasses with her best friends Gin and Tonic.

"Couldn't have been better," Harold said. "Jack was splendid – splendid."

"Splendid splendid, eh?" She elbowed her son gently in the ribs. "Well done. You're a wage-earner now."

When they were alone that night after Harold had gone out, Jack told his mother what he'd seen.

"What does it mean?" she asked; still squiffy from this afternoon, she had trouble concentrating on what he said.

"I don't know," Jack said, and he didn't. Though he could see these creatures he had no idea what they were. Elementals, he supposed from what little reading he had made about them. But what that meant he did not know. "Perhaps we should ask someone," he suggested.

"Harold might know."

"I don't want to ask him," Jack said. "*They* might hear."

"They?"

"Those things hanging from him. I don't want them to know I'm asking about them."

"But why? What harm can they do?"

"I don't know. But if you'd seen them you wouldn't want them to hear you either." Jack was adamant about that.

"Well," his mother said in a drawn-out drawl, "who do you suggest?"

"I'll think about it," Jack said, feeling suddenly tired. It had been a long, hard day and he was ready for bed.

Next day Harold was up bright and early.

"I've another five ladies booked for this afternoon and three ladies and two men tonight. Word's getting around." He rubbed his hands together vigorously. "I knew it would. As soon as they saw that eye they were hooked."

Jack nodded, though he kept his distance from Harold. Even without his third eye he was still aware of the horrible bald weasels hanging around the man's body, chattering in his ears. It gave him the creeps, so much so that when Harold strode over to him to pat him on the back in congratulations for how well he did yesterday he felt physically sick. Which Harold couldn't fail but notice. He looked at Jack queerly for a second then cocked his head to one side as if someone were whispering to him.

Jack shivered.

"I think I'm getting a cold," he stammered then left to run upstairs to his bedroom.

He didn't know what to do. Harold's scheme would make them rich; he knew that. And they needed him to make it work. But he couldn't stand the thought of being anywhere near him, not with those creatures hanging from him. His mother came into his room and gave him a hug.

"Harold's wondering what's up," she said.

Jack nodded. "I know. I could tell."

"Are you going to tell him?"

He shook his head. "I daren't."

His mother said she understood. "Should I?"

Panicking at the thought he grabbed her arms. "Please, Mum, don't. You might not be able to see them; it doesn't mean they can't hear you. I'll just have to pretend I never saw them."

"Can you?"

He shuddered but said, "I'll have to. It's too good to stop now. We need the money."

"Aye, it would be nice not to worry where the next penny's coming from. We could do with some good luck." She brightened suddenly. "Perhaps when we've saved enough we could go on holiday. A good one. Somewhere abroad. A bit of sun, sea, and sand. What do you say?"

Jack hugged her and agreed. That would be worth it. Just so long, he thought, as Harold wasn't with them when they went.

Somehow Jack managed to make himself ignore the 'filthy beasts', as he called them, that hung around Harold's body, though he couldn't help catching sight of them during the seances, however hard he tried to look away.

The money, though, kept rolling in.

"If it keeps on like this I'll end up having to pay taxes," Harold said, though Jack knew he was much too crafty for that.

Over the weeks, seeing elementals on more of the people who came to the seances Jack began to get used to them. Although he no longer felt as afraid of the creatures, they still gave him a feeling of nausea. One day he knew he would have to look into finding out what they were. He was sure someone somewhere must know. There might even be a way to get rid of them.

Three months passed and by that time Jack, turning sixteen now, was adept at what he did. So much so that he even wondered if they still needed Harold. It would be a relief to be rid of him and the things attached to him. Try as he might he could never forget about them. They worried and repulsed him. He even saw something of their sly faces in Harold's. He wondered what they were whispering to him. Whatever it was it couldn't be anything good, he was sure. Nothing good could come from creatures like that.

He mentioned this to his mother.

"But why?" she responded, shocked at his suggestion. "He's been good to us, Jack. Without him we would never have made all this money, you would never have been able to do what you have. We owe him everything."

Realising it was a mistake to mention it to her, Jack wondered what he could do. He couldn't just sack Harold. His mother would never allow that. If he got rid of him it would have to be some other way. But which?

The idea of continuing like this for years with Harold and his weasels was just too much.

Which was when he realised there was only one way. Harold would have to have an accident.

It was an idea that grew. Every day he thought of it. Every day he spent hours trying to think up plans. Some were pretty weird. Some were downright daft. None of them seemed feasible, even to a sixteen-year-old.

He would just have to watch and wait. An opportunity would present itself; he was sure. All he needed was patience, though that was the hardest part. Patience wasn't one of Jack's virtues.

"Isn't it time your boy had his first beer in a pub?" Harold said one night after they had counted the day's takings, divided them up and, in Patty's case, locked them away. Harold merely slipped his money inside a bulging leather wallet.

"He's too young yet," Patty said.

"Rubbish." Harold laughed. "How old were you when you had your first? I'll bet you were even younger than Jack."

Patty laughed as well. "I was fourteen, if you want to know. I had a Piña colada. Well, three or four actually. And was sick in the toilets."

"But you didn't wait till you were fifteen before going again?"

"No – though I sometimes wish I had. I got a taste for it soon enough."

"Well, ask the boy. He's big enough to convince any barman he's eighteen or older. He'd convince most policemen too."

"That's not the point, is it?"

Harold shrugged. "He's earning. Give him a chance to enjoy some of the money he's making. That's what I say."

Which was how Jack got invited by his mum and Harold to go out with them for a drink in their local. At first he wasn't sure, then he thought about how Harold and his mum usually got drunk when they went out and how that might give him the opportunity he'd been looking for.

"Brilliant," he said. And meant it.

It was cold and wet by the time they left the Bell and Compasses that night. A strong easterly wind was blowing, which chilled them all as they bowed their heads against the rain. If Patty's house hadn't been so close they would have booked a taxi, but it was only a five-minute walk, however unpleasant.

It was quiet, with no one on the pavement except the three of them, though the road was busy, cars hurtling past, sending out sprays of water from the kerb.

"Ignorant bastards!" Harold shouted at one car that managed to drench him with a bigger than normal spray. Jack laughed. The little man was weaving from side to side across the pavement ahead of them, intent on getting to Patty's house as quick as he could, no doubt thinking about the glasses of whisky they'd drink when they got there.

His mum just kept her head down. She hated the rain hitting her face. She was bent almost double, staring at her feet, hands pushed deep in her pockets.

Jack moved ahead of her, just behind Harold. A bus turned onto their road, its headlights almost blinding them. Behind it came a lorry. Even more spray was sent splashing into them as the bus swayed past, most of the seats inside empty.

"Mind yourself!" Jack called out. He grabbed hold of Harold's shoulders and gave him a push. The little man tripped sideways, taken so much by surprise he'd no time to react before he fell headfirst into the road, bumping off the back of the bus and straight beneath the massive wheels of the truck which bounced across him.

"He always looked after me," his mum said, wiping tears from her eyes. "To get killed tripping over his own silly feet like that, it hardly seems fair."

Jack comforted her as best he could.

"We shouldn't have drunk so much," he said. "It was an accident waiting to happen."

Jack smiled to himself. He felt as if a great weight had fallen from his shoulders, which seemed ironical, he thought. All the weight had been on Harold's after all.

Anyway, they had another seance tonight, their first without the little man.

Jack had already read through the notes he'd collected on those participating in it. By now it was easy-peasy.

Nothing to it. He felt as if he had been born to it. Soon, he might even be up to booking a place like the Theatre Royal. Who knows?

When the customers arrived, his mother showed them into the parlour where Jack was waiting. He welcomed them all, then told them about his third eye, which he knew was the reason they were here. He pulled off the bandana and opened it. For a moment he glanced at them, then he stopped and stared as something moved across his chest. It was long and thin, with the face of a weasel. It stared at his face and whispered.

THE FRAGILE MASK
ON HIS FACE

It had been a long night and Helen was glad to get away when the class finally ended. She neatly stacked her notes together, then slid them inside her briefcase.

"Do you fancy going for a drink on the way home?" Joyce asked, her own notes rolled in a rubber band and stuffed into her coat pocket.

Helen wasn't sure. It was Thursday and it was a normal workday tomorrow.

"One drink won't make you ill," Joyce insisted, almost mind-reading the reasons for Helen's indecision. "And don't tell me, after tonight's session, you don't feel like having something to help you unwind."

"I had thought of a cup of hot chocolate," Helen said, but she could feel herself giving way. Joyce's bouncy enthusiasm was almost irresistible and a sure tonic for any tiredness she might have felt a few moments before.

"One round. That's all. No more than two anyway," Joyce said, flashing a smile. "Besides, it's so cold tonight, you need something to warm you up."

The Potter's Wheel was only just off the town centre and reassuringly busy midweek. Just the usual suspects, Helen thought as she took a seat at one of the tables by the wall, while Joyce strode over to the bar. A boisterous group of old men occupied one window table, itself crowded out with full and half full pints of beer. Throughout the rest of the pub there was a dense scattering of singletons, quietly drinking their chosen solace, while a group of pool players were shouting and laughing in the next room.

"Do you think they picked this particular shade of brown so you couldn't see the nicotine stains?" Joyce asked as she deposited their drinks on the table, then shed her heavy coat. Beneath she wore a thick jumper that could have out-rivalled Joseph's coat of many colours.

"Could you not find anything more startling?" Helen asked, pretending that her eyes were being dazzled. "It was distracting enough in class."

"I'll have you know my mum made this for me and she has impeccable taste."

They broke out in laughter, then sipped their drinks, a lager for Joyce and a gin and tonic for Helen.

"Oh, oh, there's Goggle Eyes giving you the once over again."

Although, with a break from college over Christmas, it was nearly a month since they last came into the Potter's Wheel, Helen still remembered the pale young man with the goatee beard, a worn corduroy jacket and dark, curly hair, whose eyes always seemed to keep glancing their way, though he had never made any other indication of noticing their presence as he sat, slowly drinking his glass of cider.

"That's cruel," Helen said.

"You're joking. If they're not the closest things you've ever seen to goggle eyes on a man…"

Helen shook her head, though she had to admit it was an accurate description.

"I just hope he never hears you."

Joyce grinned and took another sip of her drink. "Fat chance of that with those old guys over there. They make more noise than a pack of unruly school kids."

Laughing and shouting and arguing with each other with the boisterous camaraderie born of decades of familiarity, the old men were as much a part of the pub as its outdated décor.

"Anyway, I don't think it's a good idea to make fun of him, even between ourselves. There's no saying how much he might pick up, even without hearing us."

Joyce snorted. "You're a real little scaredy cat, Helen. Anyway, he's as far through as a tram ticket, even if he did get upset."

Helen felt like saying that this wasn't the point, but it would have been wasted on Joyce, who would only be encouraged to make even more outrageous comments about him if she persisted.

"I'm surprised Tony wasn't here to meet you after class," Helen said, to change the subject.

"Tony's history now, Helen. History." There was a sneer that jarred with her humour a moment before, and Helen wondered just how historical Tony was.

"You've argued?"

"You could put it like that." Joyce pulled out a slightly crumpled pack of cigarettes and lit one. "See this? See the state of it? I've tried to give up half a dozen times since I told him to fuck off. I've fished this pack out of the bin three times already." She glanced around at the young man in the corduroy jacket. "Seen enough?" she snapped at him irritably.

"Joyce!" Helen admonished. "Keep your voice down."

There was already a lull amongst the old men, and Helen felt as if every eye in the pub was on them.

"I think I'll settle for just one drink," she said, taking a quick gulp of her gin and tonic, and tried not to cough as the harsh liquid caught in her throat.

"Helen, I'm sorry." Joyce touched her wrist. "It's just I'm still a bit raw about the bastard."

"That's all right. But you shouldn't let your feelings about him make you lash out at other people."

Joyce nodded. "I know. I said I'm sorry." She smiled

wryly. "Am I forgiven?"

For a moment Helen wondered. Joyce's mood swings tonight were catching her off balance and she really didn't feel up to it. The accountancy lesson had already taken its toll on her, what with that and worrying about the exams looming ahead of her at Easter and all the revision she would have to do, listening to Joyce's outbursts were too much just now.

"You're forgiven," she said. "Of course you are. Though there's really nothing to forgive in the first place. But I really am tired."

"One more drink," Joyce insisted. "I'll get it. Just one. Then we'll go to the bus station together. It'll be safer that way."

Which was true. There had been too many attacks against women walking the streets at night by themselves, even in built-up areas, for her to feel easy about heading for the bus station from here on her own.

"Another gin and tonic?" Joyce asked.

Helen nodded. It would help her relax, if nothing else, she thought, as the effects of her first drink began to flow through her. She glanced over at "Goggle Eyes", feeling guilty as the nickname Joyce had bestowed on him automatically came to mind, especially when she caught him looking towards her. His large, round, slightly protuberant eyes instantly turned downwards to stare at his drink, and she wondered if she caught a faint trace of a blush on his pallid cheeks. He reminded her of a very young, lightly bearded Peter Lorre; his strange eyes, far from being repellent, were oddly exotic.

"Here we are," Joyce announced, perhaps a trifle too cheerfully as she once more deposited drinks on their table.

As they talked Helen suspected that, given the chance, Joyce wanted to linger even longer in the pub, but it was nearly ten and Helen had a twenty-minute ride ahead of her even after they reached the bus station. As soon as she had finished her gin and tonic she told Joyce that she really had to be going now.

Joyce reluctantly placed her own emptied glass on the table.

"You sure?" she asked, but Helen was already putting on her coat.

Outside, the cold had become even more bitter than before, and Helen knew that winter had well and truly arrived.

"Hope it doesn't snow again," Joyce moaned as they ducked their heads into the wind. "Perhaps we should have rung for a taxi."

"I can't afford taxis. Besides, it's only five minutes to the bus station."

Joyce suddenly stopped. "Bugger and damnation!"

"What's the matter?" Helen turned her back to the wind to face her.

"I must have left my notes from tonight in the pub."

"Are you certain?"

"Positive. They were in my coat pocket. They must have fallen out while I was putting it on." An extra strong gust of wind howled around them, bringing icy cold through every gap in their clothing.

"I'll nip back for them. I'll only be a few minutes. I'll catch you up on the way to the bus station."

Helen looked down the long, deserted street, with its closed shops, sheltering behind galvanised steel shutters daubed with graffiti. Flakes of snow were beginning to spin across the road, adding to the brown smear of slush spread across it.

"I can come back with you," Helen offered. But Joyce shook her head. "I'll run and catch you up."

With that she began to hurry back to the pub, its windows beckoning with their comforting glow against the darkness.

Turning back into the wind, Helen again ducked her head against it.

Typical of Joyce to desert her like this, she decided. It wouldn't have surprised her if her friend still had her notes on her and was using their alleged loss as an excuse to get back to the pub for another drink and to order a taxi, never mind that this left Helen out here on her own. Feeling angry, Helen strode on faster, determined to reach the bus station well ahead of Joyce, even if she did intend to try and catch up and it wasn't all a lie.

She had almost reached the bus station when a car passed her. The snow had become heavier in the last few minutes and was sticking to the ground. Slush from beneath the car's tyres hissed through the air, striking her legs in icy lumps. She stopped, gasping at the shock of it. Bloody fool, she thought, angry at the driver for speeding past so close to the kerb. She looked up at it. And thought she saw Joyce's face pressed to the rear windscreen, looking back at her. But most of the glass was already covered in snow and she could have been mistaken. It wasn't even a taxi and she could think of no reason why Joyce should have got a lift in someone's car, especially from the Potter's Wheel, where they were hardly even on nodding terms with any of the regulars.

Next Thursday, though, Helen was disturbed when Joyce failed to turn up at night school. This was a crucial time for both of them, with only a couple of months to go before their exams. When the lesson had finished she asked Henry Hanshaw, their tutor, a stiff, thin-haired academic with a perpetually miserable expression on his face, if Joyce had rung in, but he told her he had no idea why Joyce hadn't come here tonight. Ringing in wasn't a requirement. They weren't schoolchildren. They or their employers had paid for this course and as far as Henry Hanshaw was concerned it was up to them if they came or not.

Stifling her irritation at his infuriating manner, Helen took out her mobile and rang Joyce's number, but there was no answer. Instead she was diverted to Joyce's answer phone facility. She left a brief message.

"Hope you are okay. Missed you tonight. If you need any help with this week's lesson, give me a ring."

She put her phone away and strode out of the austere college building. Last week's snow still lay on the ground in glaciated rucks, with ominously glistening patches of ice, which Helen gingerly avoided.

The Potter's Wheel was only a few minutes out of her way to the bus station and, though she knew Joyce was unlikely to be there, for some reason Helen felt the need for a drink before going home.

As she settled in the pub's comforting warmth, Helen remembered that she let Joyce borrow her mobile to ring her boyfriend, Tony, a few weeks ago, the battery of her own phone having gone flat. Helen looked up her record of dialled calls and scrolled down them till she found the one that was probably his. Suspecting that there may have been a reconciliation between them, which could account for Joyce's absence tonight, Helen rang Tony's number. A few seconds later she heard his familiar voice.

"Tony Farr."

"Hi, Tony, it's Helen Taylor. I'm trying to get hold of Joyce. You haven't seen her lately, have you?"

"Joyce?" Tony hesitated, as if embarrassed. "I haven't been in touch with Joyce for over a week. She's not answering her phone. She has it on divert, which I think is her way of telling me that she doesn't want to talk things over." If embarrassed to start with, his voice had very quickly adopted a tone of being aggrieved.

Ignoring this, Helen said: "She should have been at our accountancy class tonight, but she didn't turn up. That's why I'm ringing. I wondered if you guys might have made up or something."

"Fat chance of that," Tony responded petulantly.

"I'm sorry you've had an argument. I know it's none of my business, but I was sad to hear about it."

"Thanks."

"I'm beginning to get worried about Joyce. She didn't need to put her phone on divert to avoid talking to you. She could just cancel your calls when she sees who they're from. Anyway, she's not responded yet to the message I left half an hour ago."

Tony paused for a moment, probably collecting his thoughts, she supposed.

"I don't know what to suggest. I did go round to her place earlier this week, but she wasn't in. Or, if she was, she wouldn't answer her door. Though there weren't any lights on."

Helen could imagine him standing there, minute after minute, ringing the doorbell, then banging on its panels. Patience had never been one of Tony's virtues from what she knew about him.

"Perhaps she's staying with her mother," Helen suggested finally.

"Perhaps," he replied. "But I tried there as well. And, unless she's got her mother to lie for her, she's not there either."

All of which was beginning to make Helen feel distinctly uneasy. She remembered the face she glimpsed in the back of the car that doused her with slush a week ago on her way to the station. Had it been Joyce's face she saw in the back of it after all, she wondered. She preferred not to dwell too much on the expression she seemed to remember on the woman's face. As she looked back on it now she could not understand how she had failed to recognise the fear and panic that had stared back at her.

"What are you going to do now?" Tony asked. For the first time there wasn't a trace of anger, resentment or self-justification in his voice. Just worry.

"I'll ring her mum myself. I don't think she would have lied for Joyce. But even if she did, she wouldn't have any reason to lie to me."

"Will you ring me back when you've spoken?" Tony asked.

Helen smiled, despite her fears. "Okay."

After Tony had given her the number for Joyce's mother she rang off and called it.

"Mrs Wainwright? It's Helen Taylor. Joyce's friend."

The woman who answered sounded cautious, though that was probably because of the lateness of the hour. Only now did Helen realise it was nearly ten o'clock.

"Is anything wrong? Joyce hasn't had an accident, has she?"

"Not so far as I know. That's why I'm ringing. She missed her lesson at college tonight and isn't answering her phone, so I thought she might be staying with you."

"She's not staying with me, dear. In fact, I haven't heard from her for over a week. I was starting to get worried. She usually rings every day or so to see how I am."

After promising to get Joyce to phone her mum the moment she got in touch with her, Helen sat pensively for a short while, then finished her drink. She remembered that she had promised to ring Tony back, and decided that she would get another drink, then call him. At the bar she asked the landlord if he remembered her friend calling back into the pub again last week because she'd lost some papers.

The landlord scratched one ear for a moment in thought. "Curly red hair, wearing a very, *very* colourful jumper?" he asked.

Helen said that was her.

"I remember her, yes. She came back here all right. All in a-flutter, she was. Found her papers, though. They were on the floor right where you'd been sitting."

"Did she leave again straight away?"

"Probably. But I can't remember, sweetheart. There were a few people leaving about that time. Something good must have been coming on telly that night. Regular little exodus, it was."

"I don't suppose it's any good asking if you remember if she left by herself?"

The landlord beamed. "'Fraid not, my love. I was too busy with that gang over there." He nodded to the old men sat by the window. "They were ordering in another round about that time and it was all hands to the pumps, if you get my drift."

Collecting her drink, Helen returned to her table. "Goggle Eyes" was here again, drinking his cider, the glass nearly full. Though he never seemed to finish it, from what she could recall. Just took small sips, as if he didn't really care for it at all and only had it because you had to have a drink of some sort to be here, she pondered, before her thoughts inevitably returned to Joyce.

She took out her mobile and called Tony. He answered straight away as if he had been waiting. Which he probably had been, Helen thought.

"Any news?" he asked.

"Her mum's not heard from her for over a week. She's worried herself, as Joyce normally keeps in regular touch with her."

"Oh, God," Tony moaned, and she wondered if he was feeling guilty now about whatever it was that made them row. "Do you think we should contact the police?" he asked.

"I don't know," Helen said. "Would they take any notice after only a week?"

"I'll ring her office in the morning," Tony said. "If she's not been to work and hasn't rung in sick, then I think we should go to the police anyway."

Helen agreed. "Till then I don't suppose there's much more we can do."

Afterwards she stared for a few minutes at her drink, wondering if perhaps Joyce had met someone else on the rebound and was spending time with them. From what she knew of her, there was always a possibility of that. A very distinct possibility, she thought, which was one reason why she was reluctant to involve the police just yet.

"Excuse me, is your friend not going to be with you tonight?"

Helen looked up, startled. It was "Goggle Eyes". He had risen from his table and was stood next to her, contrary to her thoughts a few moments ago, having actually drained his pint. Holding the empty glass in one hand, he was on his way to the bar.

"I'm afraid not," Helen said after a pause that seemed to go on a little too long as she tried to collect her thoughts.

The young man nodded, as if absorbing the information, then took a step further towards the bar, paused, and said: "I couldn't get you a drink, could I? I see you've nearly finished."

Flustered at the unexpected offer, Helen said: "I wouldn't say no," though she regretted accepting almost at once. But it was too late. By then "Goggle Eyes" was already at the bar.

"I asked Bob for the same drink you had last time – Gin

and tonic, he said – if that's all right," the young man told her a few moments later when he returned.

"You really shouldn't have," Helen said.

"No problem. You look as if you're worried about something. Perhaps this will help cheer you up."

"Thank you, but I don't think it will, really. I'm worried about my friend. She's gone missing and no one seems to know where she is."

"That's bad," the young man said. He held out one hand. "My name's Mat Denton."

Helen took his hand lightly. It felt cold and soft. "Helen. Helen Taylor."

He smiled, looking slightly embarrassed.

"I hope you don't think I'm being presumptive, offering you a drink like that. But I feel like I almost know you, with you and your friend coming in here every week or so over the past year."

"I suppose we have become sort of familiar faces here," Helen admitted, uncertainly.

"Sort of." Mat took a tiny sip of his cider. "This friend of yours…?"

"Joyce."

"When was the last time you saw her?"

"In here. Last Thursday. We were on our way to the bus station when she remembered leaving something here and returned. She said she would catch me up a few minutes later, but she didn't."

"I was in here last Thursday," Mat said, though Helen already remembered this. She also remembered Joyce being unnecessarily rude to him.

"You don't know if she spoke to anyone when she returned, do you?"

Mat thought for a moment. "It was very busy just then. The old Grudgers, that lot over there," he added, indicating the old men, "were ordering a fresh round of drinks, and that always causes bedlam. And a few people were leaving about then, though I don't know why."

"The landlord thinks it was because something was starting on TV in a short while."

"Could have been, though I wouldn't know. I never watch television myself."

Helen added one more item to her list of oddities about him. He was the only man she could remember meeting who actually claimed that he never watched TV. What an odd thing to claim, she thought, unless he spent most of his nights here in the Potter's Wheel taking miniscule sips of his cider.

Somehow Helen managed to pass the next ten minutes in a disjointed form of conversation with Mat, till she finished her drink.

"Would you like another," Mat asked, but Helen was prepared and said: "No. I really must be on my way." She reached for her briefcase. "I have work tomorrow and it will take me at least an hour to get home."

Outside it was cold, miserable and quiet, her footsteps echoing back at her as she headed through the town centre to the bus station. She was barely halfway there, though, when she heard her mobile chime, telling her that she had just received a text message. For a moment she was undecided whether to wait till she reached the bus station before checking out what it was, but ahead was the lit doorway of Marks and Spencer, and she decided to stand there for a moment to read it.

She was surprised to see the message was from Joyce.

"hi. sorry u r worrying about me. i'm ok. meet you in a few minutes. i'll pick you up in my car. i'll explain all then. joyce."

Meet you in a few minutes? Helen looked up and down

the street. There were several cars moving, but which was hers? In fact, Helen hadn't been aware till now that Joyce even had one. It was something she had never mentioned before and had always gone home from college by bus. Anyway, Helen thought, how does she know where I'll be? Or had she been watching the Potter's Wheel? Which hardly made sense.

Undecided, Helen wondered whether to ignore the message and continue on her way to the bus station. So long as Joyce was all right that was all she was really bothered about. She wasn't interested in meeting her, certainly not at this time of night, when she was more concerned in getting home to her flat and a relaxing warm drink curled up in front of the fire, with perhaps an hour or so of watching TV to unwind, before going to bed. Why should she want to meet Joyce now to hear why she had not been to college tonight?

A large, dark car pulled up alongside her. Its passenger door swung open. Inside she could just make out Joyce's face at the steering wheel. She looked pale, almost peaky, though that could have been because of the gloominess of the car, lit only by a small white light that came on above the windscreen when the door opened.

"Come on. Jump in," Joyce barked, her voice harsh as if she had a sore throat.

When Helen hesitated, Joyce added: "It's getting cold in here. Please hurry. I'll drive you home while we talk."

An icy gust of wind, billowing down the high street and striking deep through Helen's coat, decided her, and she ducked her head beneath the door frame and let herself fall back onto the passenger seat, her briefcase on her lap. Almost immediately, as soon as Helen closed the door behind her, Joyce accelerated away from the kerb, driving quickly through town.

It was only then that Helen realised there was someone slumped on the seat behind her. She looked round as much as she could. In the intermittent light cast into the car she was surprised to see Tony Farr. His mouth jerked into a sort of smile when he saw her look at him.

"Have you guys made up?" Helen asked, disturbed at the silence that had fallen over everyone in the car.

"Later," Joyce said.

Helen stared at her as the car turned onto a road that would take them up onto the moors above the town. Darkness loomed ahead of the car as the streetlights petered out along the winding road to become randomly intermittent.

"Which way are we heading?" she asked Joyce. "Is this a short cut?"

A large farmhouse rose in silhouette against the pale, snow-laden clouds that dominated the sky. Joyce drove down a rough path that branched off the road towards it, drawing up a moment later on a snow-streaked cobblestone yard.

"What is this place?" Helen demanded. "And why have we stopped here?"

Joyce ignored her as she opened her door and climbed out of the car. Behind her, Helen heard Tony heave himself out onto the yard too, standing beside the car like an indistinct shadow.

For a moment Helen hesitated. Though she had known Joyce long enough to trust her – and had even grown to like Tony from what she had seen of him – there was something about the two of them now that disturbed her. Tony looked ill. He looked worse than ill. He looked like he seriously needed to see a doctor. His face had the grey pallor of someone with an ominously critical heart condition. Indeed, as the wind buffeted him, he rested against the side of the car as if it were too much effort to stand unaided.

"This way," Joyce said, and she led them towards the main door into the farmhouse. It swung open as she pushed it. "Inside," she went on, leading the way. A light came on in the hallway; Helen stared into the large, unfurnished room. Opposite, a flight of stairs rose into darkness. The walls were covered in old, patterned paper, stained with huge patches of damp; much of it looked like fungus. There was an overpoweringly dense smell of mould, dry rot and vermin, and Helen felt sure she would be sick if she were forced to stand inside. But Tony had moved up even closer now, pressing against her, and she stumbled forwards, up the worn flagstone steps and into the hallway, almost gagging on the smell.

Joyce, though, seemed unaffected by it. Or was she? Helen seemed to detect a change in her friend's face as she strode across the threadbare, old-fashioned carpet that only partially covered the floorboards, her heels thudding across them. She turned and faced Helen and Tony. There was a mark around the edge of her face that Helen had not noticed before, like a ragged line. Their eyes met. Joyce's looked strange, almost milky, old and oddly shrivelled. She felt suddenly squeamish as Joyce reached up to touch the line. A fingernail seemed to catch beneath it. Then slowly, deliberately she began to peal the skin from her face. It came away with disgusting ease.

"Joyce!" Helen called out, sickened at the sight of her friend's face clutched like a flimsy, cheap Halloween mask in her fingers, till she realised that the face underneath wasn't the disfigured remnants of Joyce's at all, but the blood-blotched face of Mat Denton.

For a moment she felt utter revulsion, then everything seemed to swim before her eyes. Her sense of balance deserted her, and she was aware suddenly of falling forwards, of reaching out to protect herself as the floor seemed to tip towards her.

And the cold, hard, snow-covered paving stones jarred against her arms and knees and made her cry out in pain as she slithered across them.

"Are you all right, lass?"

She looked up. Speckles of light danced in front of everything as an intense feeling of nausea washed through her and she felt the urge to be sick.

"Did you slip on the ice?"

The man's voice sounded friendly enough. An old man's voice. She looked up as he carefully took hold of one arm and helped her to her feet. The light from the window display in the Marks and Spencer store next to them looked comfortingly normal, as Helen looked around herself in disbelief. The old man held a walking stick in one hand as he gripped on to her arm with the other, a look of concern on his face.

"You took a right tumble then, lass. Have you hurt yourself?"

"I think I'm all right," Helen said, though her voice still sounded distant and she had a strange feeling of disorientation.

Just then her mobile rang. Clumsily, the palms of her hands scuffed raw by the paving stones, she fumbled through her pockets as the old man stood back and watched her with concern.

She saw before she answered her phone that the call was from Tony Farr. An image of him, grey faced and mute, stood outside the semi-derelict farmhouse, came to mind, of the strange dream or hallucination that had come over her when she fell.

"Hello, Tony," she murmured, still feeling shaken.

"Are you all right, Helen?" His voice sounded concerned, even nervous.

"I think so. Why? What made you ask?"

There was a pause. "I don't know. I just had the oddest experience. I thought you were in danger. Sounds stupid, I know."

"Did you have some kind of a waking dream?" she asked.

The pause this time was even longer. The old man who had helped her nodded, then started to walk away, carefully shuffling his feet across the icy pavement.

"How did you know?" Tony asked.

It was a question Helen could barely understand herself. Why should he have had a dream? What made her ask? And what made him ring? The more she thought about it the less sense it made.

"I just fell," she told him. "Slipped on the ice, I suppose. And had a bizarre dream about Joyce."

"That she came for you in a car?"

For a moment Helen wondered if the dream had really ended, if this was still a part of it, if she had not woken up at all. But the pain in her hands and knees was enough to convince her that this was real. Even if she were asleep this would have been enough in itself to waken her.

"What's happened to her, Tony?"

"Where are you?" he asked. "I'll come and meet you."

Feeling that this was some weird kind of deja vu, with Tony replacing Joyce this time, she told him where she was.

"Stay there," he said. "I'll be with you in less than ten minutes."

He drew up even before the first five minutes had passed, his car screeching to a standstill on the gritted road. He looked tussled and edgy when he came round to help her across the pavement to the passenger door, concerned at the scuffs on her hands and knees.

"I'll take you home as soon as we've finished," he said.

46

"But I'd like to take a diversion first."

"Up onto the moors?" Helen asked, her voice quiet. "To the farmhouse?"

"If it exists," Tony said flatly. "This sounds nuts to me. But the dream seemed so real. So oddly real."

"Our dream, you mean," Helen said.

"That's even more stupid." Even though they had not discussed their dream in detail, they both knew they had experienced the same, impossible though they knew this was.

Tony drove carefully. The moorland road had not been gritted for days and shone with a menacingly black glossiness in the headlamps. Farmhouses up here were widely scattered and lonely, grim-looking buildings, surrounded by lines of dry-stone walls and snow-covered hedgerows.

"There it is," Helen said, no trace of excitement or enthusiasm in her voice. She had been hoping against hope that they would find nothing here, that their nightmare had been nothing more than a dream. But there was no mistaking the dark, isolated, box-like building.

Tony nodded in recognition, then carefully drove down the side road towards it. He flipped open the glove compartment and took out a torch. "Are you game?" he asked. "Or would you prefer to wait in the car?"

Helen did not hesitate. "I'd be more scared waiting for you by myself."

He smiled, briefly, then climbed out. They approached the farmhouse gingerly. The icy cobblestone yard in front of it was hazard enough, even without the strong winds that buffeted them. But it was more than just this that made them walk slowly. There was an ominous presence about the unlit building, an aura that disquieted both of them, and Helen wondered if it would not have been better to have left this till daylight, perhaps after ringing the police. Although how they could explain their interest in this place without mentioning their dream she was not sure. And just how that would go down with the police she could well imagine.

At the door Tony hesitated, then he rapped on it. The sound seemed to echo through the hollow emptiness of the building. When there was no response, he rapped once more, then tried the handle.

"Locked."

With a grunt, he strode over to the nearest window and shone his torch inside. Satisfied that the place was empty, he returned to the door, took a step back, then kicked it hard with the flat sole of his foot immediately below the lock. The door thudded open explosively, bouncing against its overtaxed hinges.

The musty mixture of mould, decay and rat droppings was unmistakeable.

"How can it be so similar?" Helen murmured, as Tony shone his torch into the unlit interior. There was the staircase and the damp-raddled wallpaper, with its patches of evil-looking fungi, and the worn-out scraps of carpet that barely covered the old floorboards. It was not just similar to what they had seen in their dream, it was identical. The only element missing was Joyce.

Tony led the way inside, his footsteps hollow on the floorboards. Helen shivered. Apart from the wind, it was virtually as cold inside the farmhouse as outside on the moors.

"No one lives here," she murmured, dispiritedly, wishing she were home. "Look at the ice on the walls. There's been no heating in this place all winter."

Tony nodded. "Let's explore. If we find nothing, what have we lost?"

Though she was uneasy about this, Helen nevertheless

fell in step behind him as he moved to the nearest door. It opened stiffly, its hinges frozen. Like the hallway, this room was empty apart from cobwebs, dust, patches of mould and the inevitable scattering of rat droppings. Once started, though, they continued to move about the house, going from room to room on the ground floor, including the kitchen, with its stone sink half full of green slime and broken crockery, and cupboards littered with mouldering packets of food, abandoned here when the last inhabitants moved out what must have been years ago.

"We're wasting our time," Helen grumbled, feeling the cold numbing her hands and feet.

"Then why did we dream about it?" Tony insisted, gritting his teeth. "There must be some reason. There must."

Returning to the hallway, he started up the stairs. The landing above wavered in the torchlight; its banister rails cast elongated shadows across the high ceiling.

"Are you sure?" Helen asked. The steps creaked beneath her feet and she was sure she could smell dry rot in the air. If the floor gave way beneath them and they were badly injured they would be dead from exposure long before anyone found them here. But Tony climbed the stairs with a determination she could only attempt at mimicking. On the landing Tony paused just long enough to scan the line of doors facing them. Some were partially open, revealing rooms just as empty as those downstairs. One at the end, though, was different. It was the main bedroom at the front of the house. The door was shut fast and had a large, inverted cross painted on its varnished panels in bright red. Tony turned to Helen, his face grim. It was almost too obvious, and Helen was tempted to urge him to wait, but Tony's eyes were full of rage as he looked again at the door, its crudely painted symbol taunting him. Abruptly he suddenly levelled the torch and marched down the landing so quickly that Helen had to run to catch up.

He gripped the handle and thrust the door violently open.

The large, gloomy, dank room beyond seemed to change shape and size as the torch beam darted about it, picking out the strange symbols painted all over the bare floorboards and about its walls. Hundreds of partially used candles were littered about the edge of the room, surrounded by hardened rivulets of melted wax. But dominating the floor was an immense five-pointed star painted inside a crudely outlined chalk circle. Within the pentacle lay the body of a woman, her ankles and wrists bound with rope to metal rings fixed to the floorboards.

Tony grunted with horror as if he were about to be sick.

Dried blood had soaked into the floorboards around the woman's head. Her face, which had been savagely cut away, was an unrecognisable horror of darkened, decaying flesh, sinews, cartilage and sliced blood vessels that lay exposed across the front of the skull. Beyond the pentacle, heaped against the wall, was a pile of discarded clothes, amongst them a dirtied, brightly coloured jumper. By then, though, Helen had already recognised the curly red hair of her friend, spread amongst the dried blood surrounding the disfigured head.

This time, when reaction swept in, Helen was violently sick. Her stomach heaved again and again till there was nothing left but bile, and her throat felt scoured by stomach acids.

"The bloody, fucking, murderous bastard!" Tony grated in a voice stretched taut by emotion.

He stepped into the room. From within it, as if moving out from behind an invisible barrier, a figure emerged on the other side of the pentacle, though Helen would have sworn that a moment before there was no one there. She gasped with horror as she recognised Joyce's face, stretched like a very old waxen mask across that of the man, whose dark, distinctive corduroy jacket she recognised at once – as she did the swollen, glittering eyes that gazed out at her from between the eyelids of her friend's dead face.

Tony crouched as the figure moved towards him, too late to avoid the hammer in Mat Denton's fist. Helen watched as Denton raised it high into the air, high enough for the torchlight to pick out the matted strands of hair that were stuck to its head. Then it swung down, swiftly, bounced off Tony's upraised arm with a crack which she knew was of a bone breaking, and Tony cried out in pain.

"Oh, my God!" Helen whimpered, too shocked to move.

From somewhere close she seemed to hear a voice call to her:

"But I warned you. *I warned you!*"

Mat Denton, the dead face wrinkling across his own hidden face as his mouth twisted in a snarl, moved in on Tony as he swung the hammer down again. And again. With savage, resounding blows that beat down the weak defence of Tony's arms, then pummelled his head.

"Joyce!" Helen cried out, though she did not know why – except for the voice that had sounded so much like her friend's. "*Joyce!*"

It was then that another figure seemed to flicker within the room. Mat Denton, distracted, looked round, the fragile mask on his face becoming even more wrinkled, becoming even less like that of Joyce as he suddenly started to back away from Tony. The raw-faced apparition took a step towards him and Mat took a further step away from it. Which was when Helen heard the floorboards give way as the smell of dry rot became more intense. Mat lost his balance as his feet crashed through the weakened wood.

Dust motes rose into the air around him, grey with fungus. The translucent, faceless female figure reached out towards him, and it was as if its added weight, if such a thing had any weight at all, was enough to destroy what solidity the floorboards still had. Mat Denton cried out as, with a resounding crash, he fell through the floorboards, and through the fragile plaster and ceiling paper beneath. His arms reached out in a desperate attempt to stay his fall, but it was too late, and Helen watched in stunned silence as he gazed towards her before disappearing into the room below.

Helen was on her feet in an instant. She rushed to Tony to pull him back away from the hole and onto the safety of the landing. He was barely conscious; blood streamed down his face from where the hammer had hit him, but he was still breathing.

"We have to get out of here," she whispered to him. There was no certainty that the fall into the room below would have been enough to hurt Mat Denton seriously enough to make him harmless, and she half expected to see his plaster-covered figure return up the stairs towards them. Which was when she heard the scream. The seemingly endless, high-pitched scream of unutterable agony and terror.

Helen gripped Tony's shoulders and began to drag him with desperation along the landing towards the stairs. They had to get out of here. Get back to his car. Get out of this place completely.

At the stairs she halted. All was silent now apart from Tony's stertorous breathing.

How she managed to manhandle Tony's body down the stairs, step by step, without injuring him worse than he already was, she was afterwards unable to recall properly. Most of her consciousness was concentrated too much on listening for Mat Denton. But, eventually, what seemed like hours later, she reached the hallway. The door into the next room was still open. Lying there, amidst the debris, was Mat Denton's body.

Whether it was rage or fear that he might come round while she was still struggling to get Tony to the car across the frozen cobblestone yard outside, Helen knew she had to make sure that Denton was either dead or too badly injured to threaten them again.

It was only after she had seen him that the full horror of it all hit her. Mat Denton was all but dead. But she doubted that his fall from the room above had been what killed him, though she had no intention of staying there long enough to find out. Somehow she managed to get Tony back into his car, driving off as quickly as she could away from the farm and the moors and on into town, where she headed for the hospital. Fortunately, the blows on Tony's head had been enough to blur his memories of that night's events, and she was able to fabricate a story of him being attacked in town by a gang of thugs.

She never returned to the farmhouse. And it was months before anyone ventured there and found what remained of Mat Denton's body: by then time, decay and the ravenous appetites of the local vermin had done much to remove the full horror of what she saw that night. Of how his face had been ripped away from his head by what she knew must have been human nails; leaving only a red, raw ruin around his staring, barely living eyes - eyes which stared up in stark, paralysed terror, even in the daytime.

TERROR ON THE MOORS

As he looked out of the office window across the snow-covered roofs of the bleak East Lancashire town, with its dark church steeples and factory chimneys, their black expulsions of smoke staining the ice-grey sky, Peter Ridgeway wished that he could find some way to shorten the business he had to get through this afternoon, so that he could start off home before dark. He did not relish the prospect of the long and arduous drive ahead of him, especially with the roads as bad as they were. Only one thing could make it worse, he thought, and that was fog.

"As I was saying," Townsend continued, returning from a call in the outer office, where the staccato chattering of several typewriters seemed to perforate the air, "these figures you've provided us with will have to be checked out first before we can come to any definite decision. You realise that, of course."

Suppressing the sigh of exasperation that tempted him so much, Peter said: "I had hoped that we could have something decided upon today if possible. I'm due to be at Bacup tomorrow and it'll be next week before I can call here again." How long was he going to keep on stalling over the matter? It wasn't as if there was anything vital at stake. He pressed one hand across his forehead, soothing the tension that forewarned him of the aching to come. He hoped another bout of migraine wasn't on the way, though he wouldn't have been surprised if there was after having spent the greater part of the day with a ditherer like Townsend. How the man irritated him! He glanced at his watch. "I had hoped to be off before five," he said. It was five fifteen already, though the gloom outside made it seem even later.

"Do you have far to go?" Townsend asked with feigned

interest which Peter saw through at once, but which, despite his irritation, he decided to ignore.

"That depends on which way I go. I had thought to go by through Rochdale, then over the moors towards Rawtenstall."

Looking up from the sheets he had been leafing through, Townsend said that he wouldn't advise it. "Not tonight. There are two-foot drifts in town. God knows how deep it is up there. The road's only narrow, and bad enough at the best of times."

"But it is direct," Peter pointed out, too annoyed already at the delay to spend any time arguing with Townsend.

It was a further two hours before he could reach the stage where he could satisfactorily wind things up for the night.

As they shook hands in parting, Townsend said: "I'd better wish you good luck if you're still intent on driving across the moors. You'll need it."

Laughing dismissively, Peter stepped out into the street, walking gingerly across the hard-packed snow on the pavement towards his car. Shivering at the cold which quickly crept through his coat, he brushed the crust of snow off the windscreen. His breath misted before his face as he looked along the gloomy street. Finding his keys, he unlocked the door and climbed into the even more piercing cold inside. Starting up, he carefully drove towards the main road at the end of the street. An elderly couple, crouched forwards against the swirling flakes of snow beneath a black umbrella, crept by as he drew up at the junction. He switched on the radio; it would help to keep his spirits up on the moors, which were bleak enough, even in summer.

As he drove out of the town up the winding road towards the moors, the headlights of his car flared across the bristling bushes and trees in the hedgerow. The cat's eyes embedded in the road surface traced a luminescent line into the darkness ahead of him, before they became buried in snow further from the town, where the salt and ash petered out. Pristine and sterile and cold, the snow covered the road, showing clearly enough in its unmarked surface that it was some time since anyone had driven this way. Ignoring the sense of loneliness this imparted to him, Peter tried to concentrate on the music on the radio. There was not much for him to look at outside. What little he could make out in the pallid light of the stars that showed through rents in the clouds was almost uniformly dreary, with undulant wastes of snow on either side of the road, from beneath whose depths the only things to appear were telegraph poles and electric pylons, with the occasional stunted tree curled up like a beggar in the cold.

Gradually the road levelled out as he drove out onto the plateau-like heights of the moors. The faint streetlights of the town he had left in the valley behind him disappeared, and around him now were only the wild, bleak wastes of the moors.

Etched in a gaunt silhouette against the moonlit clouds ahead of him, a solitary signpost stood like a disused gibbet. He remembered it from previous trips this way, and knew it marked a road that led off at a tangent from the one he was on now. Where it led he did not know, since the weather had long since worn away whatever writing the sign once had inscribed upon it. Not that he had ever concerned himself about this. It was unlikely the road led to anywhere of importance or interest; few places did he knew of that were more sparsely populated than the moors, whose barren immensities seemed to have been stricken by a blight from which they had never been able to recover.

As he drove up a shallow incline towards the signpost, he was startled to glimpse someone leap out in front of him.

For a split second he saw a white blur of a face in the headlights.

There was a scream. A moment later he realised it was the tyres of his car as he stamped his foot against the brake, and it careered across the road. In an attempt to regain control, Peter pressed down on the accelerator and the car shot forwards, slithering towards the signpost. Only then did he realise just how near it was. Almost too late, he braked again, and there was a jolt as the engine stalled with a short-lived but violent shudder.

Muttering an obscenity, Peter looked round for whoever had jumped out, his hand moving to lower the window so that he could shout out his anger. The fool could have caused a bad accident, he thought, incensed with indignation.

He looked across the road as starlight glittered on the crests of snow that trailed his car like the frozen wake of a ship. Strangely, disturbingly perhaps, he could not make anyone out, though it was light enough to see if there was anyone there.

But where? Opening the door, Peter stepped out onto the snow. The pale wastes of the moors stretched dimly before him as the snow crunched under his feet. Shivering as the cold became more intense, Peter wondered how anyone could have walked this far onto the moors, even along the road; it was miles from here even to the nearest farm.

Cupping his hands about his mouth, he called out, but there was no reply, only the secretive sighs of the winds as they skimmed the moors with drifts of snow. There was not even an echo. His shouts were engulfed like a dying match in the depths of a well.

Shivering, Peter stamped his feet on the ground as he wondered whether to search around for the man's footprints, though there were none in sight. Somehow the idea of making a search did not appeal to him. Was this because he was afraid that there weren't any there after all? But he knew this was ridiculous. If someone jumped out in front of his car there would be prints. And someone had jumped out, he was sure.

Once more Peter called out, but there was no reply. This was useless, he knew. Perhaps he had been mistaken. It was dark and windy, and he was tired. It shouldn't surprise him, he supposed, that he mistook something, perhaps a shadow from the clouds, for a figure, though the stark white, featureless blue that he glimpsed had looked so like a face he could scarcely believe he had been wrong about it.

Stepping back into his car, Peter turned the ignition. There was a weary, long-drawn whine, and a sickening feeling grew inside him. Gritting his teeth, he tried again, but there was no more response than before. Again he tried, and again. He clenched his fists. It was a waste of time, he knew it. What was wrong with his car he was not sure; he was no mechanic but a salesman. All he could suppose was that the sudden stall must have damaged it in some way. There was nothing for it, he knew. He would have to abandon his car and continue on foot. It couldn't be more than four miles from here to the end of the moors, he supposed with ill-felt optimism. He remembered where the road wound down from the moors at the end there was a village. Although little more than a couple of rows of terraced houses, a shop and a garage, he was sure he would be able to get some help to continue him on his way home, even if he was only enabled to phone for a taxi. Though even four miles in weather like this was a long way, he knew. It had not been as cold as this all winter, and the inside of his car was becoming icy already.

Coming to a decision, he buttoned up his coat and climbed out. Only a few flakes of snow were falling now, but they were slowly beginning to come down in greater numbers, and he knew that another storm was on its way. He turned up his collar; it was no good worrying. The sooner he set off, the more chance he would have of reaching some sort of shelter before it got too deep.

Gradually, the snow fell thicker and thicker, thousands of feathery flakes silently blotting out the sky with an alabaster veil. With undetectable rapidity, the drifts inside the road grew deeper, drawing his stumbling feet into their yielding depths. Had it not been so bitterly cold the exertion of tugging his feet from the snow and plodding on would have soon had him drenched with perspiration. As it was, his gasps drew the icy air deep into his lungs, scraping his throat.

It seemed that he had been walking for hours; eventually he lost all track of time as the snow piled deeper and deeper on the ground and more fell down from the sky. Whenever he looked up through the obscuring flakes his eyes met the same hedgerow and willows and telegraph poles, until, in the end, he stopped looking up and walked on mechanically to conserve his strength.

When, like someone gradually waking up from a fitful sleep, he finally came to pause and look around, it was to the bewilderingly alarming realisation that he could no longer recognise his surroundings. The road had gone, and there was only the endless snow stretching out into the fog-like gloom. The telegraph poles, the pylons and everything else he knew to surround him on the road, and which he now expected to see, were gone. When or how they disappeared, he did not know. Even as he looked his tracks were being blurred into oblivion by the snow still falling, and he knew that to attempt retracing them was a futile task. Yet what else could he do? To go on would gain nothing. The moors continued for scores of miles and ended only in an equally barren and desolate range of hills. To make matters even worse, the moon, which had so far provided some sort of light, despite the incessant snow, was sinking swiftly and would shortly pass beyond the rim of the horizon. A greater gloom was already spreading across the wastes.

As he stared indecisively into the void, he thought he saw something move. It was faint, almost furtive, on the edge of his sight. As he turned to face it, whatever it was seemed to draw away from him. He could not make out what it was; it was just a dim grey blur in the distance, like a grease smear dabbed across glass. He wiped his eyes, as if the smear were on them; they were beginning to sting as it was, with tiredness and strain. But it did no good.

"Hello there!" he shouted.

Startling him, the shape suddenly started to run away from him, and he could tell it was a man. He knew that for certain as he caught the vague impressions of out-jutting arms and legs as the figure clumsily clambered across the snow.

"Wait!" Peter bellowed. "Don't run away! I'm lost! Can you help me?"

But for all the good it did he might as well have cracked a whip at the man's heels. Couldn't he understand what he was shouting to him? "Wait!" Peter called out again, but the cold seemed to splinter in his throat as he set off in pursuit, and he had to stop running to cough. He wiped tears from his eyes with the back of his hand. This was no good, he knew it. He couldn't run in this stuff. He was exhausted.

Looking up, he watched the wavering outline of the figure. As he stared through the darkness, he thought he could make out the vague impression of an open coat flapping in the wind about him.

Choking back a further bout of coughing, Peter forced

himself to start trudging on after the figure again, pace by pace, one step at a time.

He glanced at his watch. It was twelve fifteen. By now his wife would be getting frantic about him. She would have phoned Townsend - they had his home number in their address book - and have found out just how long ago he set out. But thoughts of this type could not claim his attention for long: the cold was too bitter, and the aching tiredness of his arms and legs were far too insistent.

A few moments later, wiping all remaining thoughts of his wife's concern from his mind, he saw a darkish, hulking shadow appear from the gloom of the distance, swallowing the smaller, shadow-like figure in its looming mass. As he hurried towards it, Peter could see the buttressed walls and high-peaked roof of a farmhouse slowly taking shape in front of him, its unlit windows gleaming like lead in the gloom.

Was this where the man he'd been following lived? Cautiously, Peter stepped towards it across the blurred impression of a cobbled lane. Looking around, he couldn't see the figure anymore. When or where he had gone, he did not know, unless he'd gone into the building.

"Hello!" Peter shouted, but there was no reply. Dismissing the man from his mind, he struck a match and peered through one of the ground floor windows into the farm. Its glass was rimed with thick grey veins of frost that distorted and blurred the light as it shone across the back of an old armchair pushed up against the windowsill inside. The deep layer of mouldering dust on top of it showed how long the place had been empty. If nothing else, though, it could provide him with some sort of shelter for the night, he knew, somewhere where he could escape from the full bitterness of the cold.

Stepping around the building, he found a barn and some fencing further on, and the rusting fragments of several farming implements. How long the place had been deserted was hard to tell, though it must have been for some considerable time. As he glanced across the roof, he was relieved to see that it looked reasonably intact and didn't appear to be in an imminent state of collapse. This was his only worry about it, since he knew that if he had an accident here, he would have very little chance of getting any help. Even in summer he doubted if more than a few hikers ever ventured here.

When he tried to push open the front door, he found that it was locked - either this, he thought, or the hinges had rusted solid. But this did not worry him much, since the wood was rotten, and a good push would easily force it in. Stepping back a pace, he launched himself at it, hearing the wood give way beneath him. A moment later he swayed into the unlit hallway. Involuntarily, he coughed. There was a mustiness to the air that seemed to lie thick inside his mouth and throat like a layer of film. It was as if he had breathed in a mouthful of cobwebs. He spat on the tiled floor as he looked around at the back of the door. A rusted, finger-like bolt had been torn from the discoloured wood when he forced it open. He looked down the hallway in the guttering light of his match. At the opposite end there was another door that let out to the back of the house. This too was locked with a heavy, rusted, iron bolt. He wondered how whoever locked it up had got out. Then he shrugged, as the open door behind him let in the wind, circulating its cleaner air into the farm as he lit another match, its dim light revealing the blotched wallpaper on the walls, spotted with mould. Opening a door beside him into what he presumed to be the living room, he wondered if he could spend the night in a place like this. But the only alternative was the moors, and he knew there was really no choice. Not now.

He looked across the room at the fireplace. There were a few small lumps of coal in the grate. Several more were heaped in a battered scuttle beside it. Some minutes later, using these and a copy of *The Daily Telegraph*, which was folded in his overcoat pocket, he managed to get a fire going. Drawing up one of the huge armchairs, he swept the rat-droppings off its mildewed seat and sat down on it, holding out his hands towards the minuscule flames that were slowly starting to writhe through the smoke that lingered about the coals.

Now that he was at last reasonably comfortable, with some semblance of warmth gradually beginning to circulate from the fire, he wondered where the man he had been following had gone. It seemed strangely suspicious that he should have inexplicably appeared on the moors when he was lost and led him here, at the same time making sure that he did not get near enough to see him properly, before disappearing again. Was he some kind of hermit, perhaps? It wouldn't have surprised him to find an odd kind of crank or eccentric hiding here. A place like this probably attracted oddballs of that sort, he supposed. It was lonely enough. The only niggling thought that worried him, though, was the suspicion that both he and the idiot who ran out in front of his car and got him stranded here in the first place were one and the same. If they were, it was almost as if he had planned to get him here, though the idea seemed too fantastic for him to give it any serious consideration. There were too many coincidences, he thought. No one could plan out something like this and be sure of being able to carry it out as he intended, especially in weather like this.

Drawing his legs onto the chair, Peter decided that the best thing now was to attempt to get some sleep so that he would be as fresh as possible in the morning. At first light, he would be able to set out across the moors and find his way back to the road.

He was so exhausted it was not long before he finally slept. It was not a deep sleep, though, nor restful since the chair was too cramped for any kind of real comfort on it. It was as he fitfully turned to rest his head on the other side, when he suddenly found himself listening to the creaking tread of someone approaching him across the bare floorboards in the room. Instantly, he was fully awake.

Throwing himself from the armchair in alarm, he rolled onto his feet to face the intruder. His hands fumbled into his coat for the box of matches. The fire had died into a few crumbling ashes that cast off only a dim red light that barely reached the edges of the hearth. Finding a match, he struck it. As it flared up, he saw that the room was as empty as before. No one was here. No one except himself.

Giving vent to a long-drawn sigh of relief, Peter reached down beside the fireplace and tore up some more pages of *The Telegraph*, pushing them under the dying embers. It took only a few minutes before he managed to revive the fire once more and had added a few more lumps of coal to it, and he was able to look around the room more carefully in its light. The hall door was partially open, though he thought he'd closed it. Could someone have started to come in the room? The footsteps stopped, he remembered as soon as he leapt off the chair. Unless, of course, the sounds had not been coming from the floorboards of this room but from one of the rooms upstairs. Perhaps the man he followed here had taken shelter in the house as well. Perhaps he lived here.

Unsure whether he should try to find out if there was anyone else in the farmhouse with him, Peter got up and began to look around the room he was in. Noticing a small, glass-fronted, old-fashioned bookcase by one wall, squeezed up next to a web-draped ruin of a writing desk (where, no doubt, he imagined, the farmer used to sit when he did his accounts) Peter stepped towards it, wondering if there was anything still left in a fit condition amongst the books crammed in it. Now he was fully awake once more, he needed something to occupy his mind till he felt like sleep again. It was still only half past two, and there were hours yet to go till dawn. Too long to sit staring at the fire or the decaying shambles of the room.

Kneeling beside the bookcase, he lit a further match and glanced along the titles of the books. Apart from a few agricultural works and a dog-eared *Plain Man's Guide to Bookkeeping*, the rest seemed to be printed in either Latin or German with heavy bindings, sometimes of leather, and sometimes reinforced with strips or bands of iron or copper. He pursed his lips as he attempted to read one or two of their titles out loud. *Enchiridion, Crih Yussus Cathelas'ytca, Unaussprech-lichen Kulten...*"

He frowned, as he carefully withdrew one of the obviously fragile volumes. Its wrinkled binding seemed almost glued to those on either side, and he had to push them in as he pulled it free. At last it rested in his hands, limp and clammy, with its peculiarly flesh-like binding lying stickily on them. It was much decayed, and he doubted if he would even be able to part its pages, much less read what was printed on them.

Placing the book on the floor in front of the fire, where its light would enable him to see it properly, he gently prised its pages open. To his surprise, he found that it was a book on what appeared to be the occult or mythology. Which of the two he wasn't sure. Some of the heavy, crinkled pages were filled with elaborately detailed etchings. But they were too discoloured for him to be able to make them out properly, though he could tell they were intended to portray various kinds of grotesque creatures: hydras and griffins, he supposed, things of that nature. Whoever owned this house before it became derelict must have obviously been a deeper man than he would have normally expected to find living in these inhospitable parts. He sighed. For all its oddity, this didn't provide him with anything that could relieve the tedium of the long, bleak hours until dawn. He did not relish the idea of trying to wade through some eighteenth-century treatise on demonology printed in Latin - even if the books had been in a fit condition to read at all.

Returning to the bookcase in the hope of finding something more interesting, Peter glanced along its shelves once more, but without seeing anything he could possibly sit down and read. Looking instead at the writing desk, he saw that its lid had been broken in, and seemed to have been partly burned at some time. He tore off the rest of it and peered inside, twisting his lips as he made out the remains of a rat's mummified skeleton.

Using a piece of wood broken from the lid, he pushed the fragile bones out of the way, to reveal a cardboard box of candles. At least these would help to brighten the place up once he'd got them lit. He shook his head, puzzled, as he took a few out and placed them on top of the bookcase. Every one of them was black. Black wax? Wasn't that the kind of thing they used in Satanic Masses? He wasn't too sure, since the only reading he'd ever done of the subject was confined to the newspapers and a couple of Sunday supplements.

If he were right, though, it would tie in with the books and, to some extent, explain why the owner of the farm had come to such a lonely place. Where better to hold whatever rites they performed than deep in the deserted moors about here?

Remembering the man who led him here, Peter wondered if he could have any connection with the last owner of the farm. Unless, of course, he was the owner himself, his mind so degenerated by whatever vile practices he'd been indulging in that he was almost insane. Peter frowned; although he'd assumed the man was probably no more than a harmless eccentric, this cast a darker, more worrying aspect upon him, and an aspect which he found peculiarly disturbing. Black Masses, besides a great many other things, involved blood sacrifices - or so he had always been led to believe. The idea of a deranged Satanist prowling about the place disquieted him as he looked about the ugly room, as the candles he'd lit cast wavering shadows about it.

Wishing now that he had left the bookcase alone, Peter looked through the doorway into the hallway outside. Unlike before, the vast, empty darkness of the farm's cavernous interior seemed suddenly sentient with an aura of potential menace, the chill that the fire behind him had partly relieved perceptibly more pronounced as he listened above the cracklings of the burning coals to the minute creaks and groans of the house.

This was no good, and he knew it. He had no other choice but to remain inside the house till morning. It would be certain suicide to go out now and attempt to find his way across the moors, especially with the coldest hours of the night yet to come.

But he knew he couldn't rest if the possibility remained of someone entering the room he was in while he slept and attacking him. Closing the hallway door, he pushed one of the armchairs up against it. Just to make absolutely sure, he wedged a couple of the heavier books beneath its casters, testing it to his satisfaction afterwards. Reassured by this, he settled himself once more before the fire.

Although he could not have felt less like sleep when he sat down, it was not long before sheer tiredness and the howling of the winds about the house lulled him as he stared at the fire. It was just as well, he thought drowsily, as the flames lost shape in his bleary sight. It was too long till daybreak to stay awake. Sleep would shorten it, he knew, as he drew his coat about himself and closed his eyes. Apart from the hushed lowing of the wind and the occasional creak of old, decaying timbers in the farm, it was silent.

As he slept he dreamt he was in a large, dark room, replete with silk covers and a huge, unlit chandelier. Lying on a couch, Peter seemed midway between wakefulness and sleep, a closed book lying on his lap.

There was a knocking at the door behind him. Looking over his shoulder, he called out: "Come in," before returning his attention to the twisting flames in the fire. He heard the door open as someone stepped in, crossing the room quickly towards him. A draft blew in with whoever had entered. Peter shivered at the sudden cold.

"What do you want?" Peter asked. The chill embraced him, blotting out the heat from the fire completely.

Feeling suddenly nervous, Peter turned to face whoever had entered the room. For a moment, though, he could not make anyone out. It was as if his eyes could not focus properly. A mist-like sheen obscured his sight.

As the cold became more intense, numbing him, he stared into the myopic mist that was drawing about him. His lips strained into a disbelieving leer of fright as he made out the whitish, doll-like head that loomed through the shadows, its round eyes glimmering dull and yellow into his. In a fit of panic, Peter broke the paralysis that had gripped him, and flung his arms before his face, barring the vision from his sight. He cried out. Something cold - icy cold - seemed to wrap itself about his throat, tightening. He was being choked, he realised. Gagging, he tried to get to his feet to fight the thing off. But he couldn't budge the weight that was pressed against him, forcing him back onto the couch. His eyes bulged as he stared unwillingly, but unavoidably, at the stark white face in front of him. It seemed unreal. Too round. Too blank. Too white.

He barred his teeth as he fought to breathe. Although he could not feel anything tangible about his throat, his flesh was being crushed by whatever was holding him. The face, swimming through a mist of nausea, came nearer towards him. He saw a small, round mouth, its bleached lips puckered with cracks and wrinkles radiating from it. Nearer. Nearer. This couldn't be real. It wasn't happening to him. It couldn't be! It couldn't! Peter fought against the pain in his throat as he reached up to tear whatever was grasping him away. It must be a nightmare, he thought to himself - a dream.

Closing his eyes, as he strained to cry out and scream, he forced himself to resist the delirium that asphyxia was pounding through his bursting head. He screamed. Like a dagger blade drawn across glass, he heard it screech through the silence.

The face touched his. In that instant the dream became darkness - cold, thoughtless, deathlike darkness, that seemed to go on and on and on...

...through eternity.

A thin beam of cold sunlight, piercing the gloom of the living room, shone into Peter's eyes as he awoke. Clenching them shut against the glare, he adjusted his position on the floor as he groaned at the pain. An aching stiffness pulsed through his neck as he moved his head. Opening his eyes once more, he felt for the edge of the armchair, lifting himself onto it. The fire had gone out, and he felt frozen. Snow framed most of the grimy windows, glowing brilliantly white against the sunlight.

Coughing harshly, Peter glanced at his watch. It was 9.15. He felt an instant sense of relief that the night had ended. Despite the seemingly interminable empty blackness following his dream, memory of it was still fresh in his mind -

nauseatingly fresh. He felt at his throat, wincing as his fingers touched the bruised flesh around it. It seemed raw, as if he had really been attacked. Puzzled, he looked towards the hallway door. To his surprise, it was open. The armchair he'd pushed behind it had been moved halfway across the room; the books, wedged beneath its casters, had been torn apart by it.

Shaking his head, Peter told himself that it couldn't be true. It couldn't. He would not allow himself to believe it was possible.

Taking a grip on himself, Peter made his way to the hallway. His legs felt so weak they could scarcely support his weight, and he had to hold onto the various pieces of furniture in the room to stop himself from falling. But this was because of the cold, he told himself. All he needed was some fresh air and some exercise to get his circulation going again, and he would be all right.

Taking a deep breath, Peter looked out through the open door across the farmyard towards the moors. It had stopped snowing now, and the smooth layers that had settled seemed to stretch out endlessly before him to the sky.

The pain in his throat seemed to worsen suddenly, and he felt at it, carefully. Had someone really tried to choke him while he slept? He really felt as if someone had grabbed hold of him. It couldn't have felt any worse if someone had, he was sure. Nor could he have felt more drained than he did.

He looked again at the hallway door. Someone must have pushed it open; he knew. No matter how much he might have preferred to ignore it, he could not truthfully believe he'd done it himself in his sleep.

Peter glanced up the stairs that led from the hallway into darkness. Shuddering, he turned again to the farmyard, but he couldn't go out. Gritting his teeth in an attempt to control the sudden trembling that rippled through him, he returned to the living room. One of the black candles he lit during the night was still burning. Picking it up, he went back into the hallway. He knew he would have to find out if the man who led him here was upstairs. He knew he would have to find out. If he didn't, he'd never know if he might have been attacked or not during the night. Even though he knew he was probably letting his overwrought imagination get the better of him, Peter knew as well that he had to find out.

Holding the candle before him, he went to the stairs, glanced up them once as the gloom dispersed before the candlelight, then slowly, carefully, he started to climb up, the bare, wooden steps groaning under his feet. At the top, he paused for a moment as he glanced along the landing. In the wall facing him a narrow window had been boarded up. Letting in no light, only the candle revealed the claustrophobic piles and drapes of webs that covered the mould-pocked walls, hanging in dim grey arches across the ceiling and obscuring it from sight. They seemed to muffle the sounds of his footsteps as he walked along the landing, making him think of the walls and ceiling of a padded cell that had fallen into decay.

As he looked along the doors, he noticed an inverted crucifix nailed to one. Stained brown, it was surrounded with the faded impression of a pentacle, symbols and marks positioned between its points. Reaching for the door handle, Peter pushed it. There was a moment's resistance, then the door swung open.

Thick though the webs had seemed outside, they filled the room with even greater profusion, and even if the window inside had not been boarded up like the one on the landing, Peter doubted much light could have entered it. Cautiously, he stepped inside, wading through the dust-laden webs that were strung like nets across the floor. As he parted those in front of him, he noticed a bed. He frowned, feeling suddenly afraid. Someone was lying on the bed, though the webs surrounding it had not been disturbed for years. He sniffed the air suspiciously, slowly drawing towards the bed. He knew that whoever lay on it had to be dead and was therefore prepared for what he considered to be the worst. But, as he came nearer and looked at the motionless body, he felt a sickening wave of horror sweep over him. Its rounded, grotesque doll-like head was puffed beneath its off-white flesh as it stared with yellowed eyes at the ceiling, its open mouth parted in what he could have only described as a look of repletion.

"God, no!" Peter muttered, recognising the hideous vision from his dream. He spun round, kicking a chair by the wall. Acting on instinct, Peter put the candle on a table by the bed and took hold of the chair, kicking out one of its legs. The rotten wood splintered and gave way beneath his foot. Bending down, he tore off a jagged length of wood, brandishing it towards the abomination on the bed. Knowing that he would have to act fast, Peter raised the dagger-like weapon in the air and thrust it down at the swollen head. The repulsively pulpy flesh parted beneath it, and the sharp wood sank deep into the soft interior of the skull. As it did so, Peter saw a pale grey vapour begin to seep from its mouth. It passed through the air towards the doorway, growing denser as it did so. Releasing the chair leg, Peter looked back as a darkening mass began to form, blocking the door.

A whimper of despair trickled from Peter's lips as he realised his mistake. The body on the bed had never moved - nor could it - it was only a husk. It was not this that lured him here and attacked him during the night. He screamed, collapsing to his knees as he stared at the blank white, doll-like head appearing in the doorway as the vapours condensed, its open, serrated, sucking mouth moving towards him.

THE SHADE OF APOLLYON

I had been expecting Updike all night and expecting him with a feeling if disquiet. As soon as I heard his car pull up in the rising fog outside, the characteristic slamming of its door, and his heavy footfalls along the asphalt path towards my house, this disquiet gave way to the irritation I had been hopelessly trying to subdue.

Updike was a large man, tending in his later years to too much weight, though his deep red face lost none of its aggressive stubbornness; firmness of purpose, some might say, though others could interpret it less flatteringly, though perhaps more perceptively, as petulance. This latter definition seemed certainly more accurate when he stepped in, his pale blue, glassy eyes gliding with an amused air of contempt across the packed bookshelves that covered most of the walls of my study as I showed him in.

"Still hanging onto the same old gibberish, I see," he remarked, withdrawing one of the volumes. Its pages crackled beneath his rough fingers as he flicked his way through it. "Three hundred years old?" he asked, smiling faintly. "*The Tract of Calvanicus,*" he continued, not waiting for my reply. "You know, if he were alive today, he'd be lucky to stay out of an asylum. It surprises me, apart from the book's antiquity, why someone should want to own such stuff as this."

"Such stuff as that," I said, trying to control the irritation I felt boiling inside me, "is invaluable in my research."

Updike chuckled. "You'll have to watch out," he said, "or one day they'll be putting you in an asylum in his place. You can't seriously pretend that anything of value can be gained from sources as disreputable as this."

"You know very well that it can. And is."

"I wish I did. Sometimes," he said. "But I never could blinker myself that well. The truth will out, as they say. Or, at least, it does for some of us." He laughed quietly, passing his attention along the shelves, though he was obviously only taking a superficial interest in the titles he was looking at.

By some exertion of will I ignored the sarcasm of his remarks, stepping to the curtains and drawing them. Already streetlamps were twinkling like stars in the gloom.

"In your letter you stated that you wished to talk to me about something," I said, more as a challenge than as a reminder. Even courtesy seemed beyond all tolerance, much though I detested being visible annoyed by his attitude. This was obviously what he intended, and, although I could not see any purpose in it, I had no desire to be manipulated in any way by him. I cast my mind back over the last few months and the bitter course of our protracted argument in *The Open Mind*. Started by attacks upon an article of mine in the magazine on the stone images of Paasch Eyland, it had quickly gathered in vehemence into a veritable feud where in stood - or so it would seem from his remarks - for the blind acceptance of every superstition and myth that the fevered minds of men had ever formed, and Updike for the calm collectedness of the agnostic truth-seeker - whom I had referred to as a "seeker without eyes".

Looking down at a shrivelled Hand of Glory, Updike said: "I thought that now, once and for all, we could settle our little dispute. Neither of us has given much ground, and it hasn't done either of our standings much good to bicker like a pair of guttersnipes in the press, even in the select press that we've used."

This seemed too much like a pre-rehearsed and typically insincere speech of his to me, and I looked at him sceptically. "Do you really think we can settle anything between us tonight?" I asked. "And what, in any case, would be the point? We have no common ground on which to argue any further than we already have. As far as I'm concerned we could discuss the subject from now until daybreak, and if our discussions so far in *The Open Mind* haven't settled anything, I can't see how any further discussion now will help. It would be a complete waste of time. Why you even bothered to contact me about this, I do not know."

"Perhaps because, unlike yourself, I don't like to leave an argument unsettled," Updike said, laughing - it was a dry, cold, humourless laugh. Even as I watched him, I could sense the arrogance that motivated every muscle in his face.

"That's as may be," I replied, "but I cannot afford to waste time in trying to persuade you that there are such things as demons."

"There's no need to try and persuade me by argument," he said, his eyes glinting with supercilious amusement.

"What do you mean?" I asked.

He waved his hand about the room at the books. "You could show me every book in the world that has ever been written about spooks and hobgoblins and I would still say to you, as I already have, that they've all come from the mind." He tapped his skull significantly, smiling. "That's it, you know, the mind. *In the mind*. Spooks have never come from anywhere else but a possessed mind. Yes, from the mind."

"If that's all you want to say," I replied icily, "then you need hardly have bothered coming at all. I *know* that such things as demons exist. And all the sarcasm in the world could not change my mind."

Updike shrugged. "You say you know they exist. All right, prove to me that they do, if that's so."

"And how would you like me to do it?" I asked.

"By invoking some demon for me to see that such things exist."

"Don't be stupid. If you knew the dangers such a thing would involve you wouldn't even make the suggestion."

"But you could do it?" he asked mockingly.

"I could. But I wouldn't. Such a thing would be far too dangerous. I place a higher value on my sanity *and* my soul than you obviously on your own, and I would not risk them with an invocation, no matter how great the reason might be for doing so. And to convince you that demons exist is nowhere near a strong enough reason for me even to contemplate doing such a thing."

"It sounds to me, quite honestly, as though you're trying to get out of it. You say you could prove to me they exist, but you won't because it's far too dangerous. Is that so?"

"You've just about summed it up accurately," I said.

He laughed, leaning towards me, his flushed face nearing mine. As I smelt his breath I realised at last why he was acting as outrageously as he was, since it was absolutely foul with alcohol. Incensed with indignation that he should have had the effrontery to come to my house in that condition, I realised I could not tolerate what he had done without repaying him in some way. He wanted proof that demons existed. I would give him that proof, and in a way that would not bring even the slightest risk to either him or me. I would delude him as only a self-deluded boor like Updike should be deluded and shake him of his self-opinionated self-satisfied and overblown egotism. I would reveal to him the Shade of Apollyon, the terrible Angel of Death.

Easing away the tension that my irritation had been creating, I nodded my head, saying: "Very well. I'll prove to you that such things as demons exist."

Updike's eyes opened in disbelief, half mocking me even now, though there was the slightest shadow of doubt. "You'll invoke something?" he asked. "Despite the risks you were telling me about only a moment ago?"

"I said I would prove to you that demons exist, and I will. However," I added, "it will be an arduous task and I could do with some refreshment first before I start. Would some coffee be fine with you?" I asked, stepping towards the hallway door.

Evidently, as I had hoped, feeling the more unpleasant aftereffects of too much alcohol, Updike said that he would. "But you'll have to work hard to convince me there are such things as spooks," he called as I made my way towards the kitchen. I smiled to myself, beginning to enjoy in prospect the harmless but satisfying revenge I would soon be able to perpetrate upon him for all his ill-mannered insolence. In his coffee I added a few grains of a special hallucinogenic powder I had obtained several months before in order to make him more susceptible to the suggestions I would shortly begin to make to him. Within ten minutes of my return Updike was lying unconscious in a disturbed sleep, his drained cup lying on the floor beside him.

Quickly I dragged him onto a hard wooden chair, fastening him to it with leather belts from my wardrobe upstairs. Then I waited till he began to come round. Straight away I started to swing a ring back and forth before his eyes. In my studies into the occult I had spent some time studying hypnosis. Before his mind had risen from the mire into which it had been plunged by the drug, Updike was beginning to stare with an unusual concentration at the swinging, glittering circlet, listening without movement except for the regular motions of his chest as I spoke to him. Carefully I led him down into the dark recesses of his sleeping, drug-filled mind.

Within a few minutes Updike was helpless, a slave to my every whispered command. His face stared blankly before him, his eyes unblinking, his body rigidly still. Carefully I prepared the way for the "proof" I had promised to give him. I told him that he would and must believe every word that I said to him, that everything I said would be the clear, indisputable truth. I asked him if he would do this. He nodded his head. I decided that now I could begin. I would teach him that his narrow-minded scorn and derision of the occult was not only ridiculous but potentially dangerous as well. I would teach him also that he could not trick his way into my house to insult me with his drunken ramblings and that his mind - of whose crystal clarity he was so naively proud - could be as putty in my hands when I chose it to be. I would scare his soul to the brink of insanity, to the outermost edges of Hell.

Initially, I began to disassociate him from his usual surroundings. Being a matter of fact, down-to-earth type of person is all very well, I thought, as long as one is in one's customary surroundings, where one's values, furthermore, are all taken for granted and where there is nothing to shake them.

So, with a few choice words, I transported him from our cosy land to the Middle East, describing for him the strangely cramped streets that wormed their ways untidily between tall, sun-bleached buildings of dazzlingly white stone, the divers stalls of fruits and spices, describing for him their various wares, the bright coloured cloths, the raisins and dates, the obscurely shaped pots, the glittering daggers and wicker baskets. And then the people, the wandering tourists with their cameras and sunglasses, and then the Arabs, brown and rugged like the bark of old trees, each jabbering volubly in their alien tongue. And then the oppressive heat and fatigue that were slowly crushing his body.

As I told him of this, Updike's face began to sweat as if he could actually feel the sun's blistering heat beating unmercifully on him. He began to look haggard and tired. Success staring back at me from every weary aspect of his face, I continued, telling him of how he pushed his way through the bustling crowds, finally breaking away from them to enter a small, darkly shaded bazaar. It was a curious shop in many ways. Around its matted walls were hung its various wares, the swords and daggers in their leather scabbards, scimitars and khandas and the deadly kris, to carved boxes of finely grained wood, baskets piled up into insane pyramids about the floor between the shop door and the dingy, unvarnished table that served as a counter and as a depository for books that lay like ancient mummies in a withered semi-preservation amongst the dust.

I told Updike how he called for service, and how a bent old man, as insubstantial and frail as cobwebs, scuttered towards him from the cave-like doorway at the back.

Then Updike - by my whispered commands - decided to buy a statuette of jade, carved finely into the shape of a squatting demon. It was a most inordinately uncouth object: bulbous and ugly, entwined tentacles were circled about its onyx base. It was an evil object, its grotesque face embossed with purest hate. All of these features Updike saw within his mind: the talons, the fangs, the shimmering scales, and the grossly elongated, primordial, claw-tipped wings that curved from the statue's monstrous shoulders.

Updike's face twisted with undisguised disgust. He abhorred the statue, detesting it completely. From now on I knew I would have to act with utmost care. To make him react too favourably towards the unctuous object could break the Mesmeric chains festooned within his mind, awakening him back into reality.

Instead I told him that it was valuable, worth many

times more than the pathetic trifle asked for it by the Arab. I told him that the old man did not know its true value. That he would make a great deal of money out of it later on. That, despite its obscene hideousness, it was really quite a rare and precious antique, a find that would fill his pockets later, just as it filled his mind with disgust just now.

Thus, by appealing to his materialism, I made the purchasing of the damnable object acceptable to him. And he began to smile in pride. Despite my anger I too smiled as I watched him stare so pleasurably at the empty air in front of him.

I told him then of his leaving the shop, bidding farewell to the bowing shopkeeper, then hurrying back up the crowded street towards his hotel at the top of the shallow hill, its blank but new walls thrusting proudly against the shimmering blue expanse of the sky.

Without pause he entered, passing the reception desk on his way towards the lift, going up to his floor. He looked along the closed white doors, the varnished floor. Room number 7...8...9...10. Yes, this was it: 11.

I told him of his opening the door and entering his room and placing the statuette on the chest of drawers opposite his bed, standing back for a moment to admire his prize - to admire its monetary value, of course. Then I told him of the fast approach of dusk, as the sky became tinged with mauve, and shadows lengthened and merged into a dull mass that seeped over everything.

As it darkened, so Updike lit the lights beside his bed. Black shadows flickered, undulating in the numerous niches and crannies around him. And the statuette, by subtle suggestions, began to appear more frighteningly spectral, as the pulsating shadows gave it a strange, sub-animation, a vague, unhealthy semblance of life.

Of course, even though Mesmerised, Updike scoffed at

the uncanny fears settling in his mind, dissipating them. But I was insistent. Perspiration glistened on his broad forehead. Becoming pale, he drew his lips tight against his teeth. But still he scoffed. And still I was insistent, describing for him the obnoxious and suspicious changes that seemed to be ravaging the squatting statuette, the peculiar way in which its gnarled face seemed to change expression, the way its sharp-toothed mouth seemed to move, opening wider and leering hideously at him, the ways its fingers seemed to crawl about the onyx base like worms, wriggling repulsively, and the way its sagging chest seemed to swell and shrink, almost as if it were breathing, but carefully so as not to be noticed. And he saw these things, though he did not understand them. But he feared them. Against his will, against all logic, he felt afraid! Beads of perspiration threaded his brows as he strained his eyes in the lamplight.

I told him to pick up the statuette, to study it carefully, to ascertain whether what he felt he had seen happening really had. I told him to peer at it closely. I suggested that he should look at those strange scratches about its slab-like base. "Or are they merely scratches?" I asked, for certainly they looked as if someone, half frantically, had scrawled upon it with something sharp, perhaps in rage... or fear?

Updike's brows became furrowed with concentration and perplexity. I told him to look closer at the marks. Were they letters? Were they? He bent his head down, narrowing his eyes. What did they spell out? What?

"A"... Yes, yes, he could make out an "A", even though it was faded by age and wear to an extreme. And then a "P", and an "L", two "L"s. Slowly I spelt out the dreadful name... Slowly... slowly: "A-P-O-L-L-Y-O-N"... Apollyon! At once he knew this was what the statuette was called. But what did it mean? What was it? A God? A demon? Neither? Both? Was it a fallen angel? But, yes, I reminded him, that was it.

Apollyon, the Angel of Death, the Plague Scourge, the Grim Reaper... the Devil!

I told him to be careful. "Make sure it is just a block of cut stone." But he was unwilling. He felt afraid.

Noticing this, I told him to put it back on the drawers. He did so gladly. The thing troubled him abominably, filling him with strange doubts and fears.

I told him of his getting ready to retire, of his climbing into the great, well-sprung bed. What was it that made it seem so like a tomb? And of his drawing back the mosquito nets. What was it that made them seem so like funeral drapes, darkening in the gloom?

As the night progressed I told him that he was unable to sleep, feeling restless though tired. In the half light of the glimmering gas lamps, he stared at the wall opposite. Slowly his eyes descended towards the cross-legged idol, looking unwholesomely green and translucent on top of the drawers. In the darkness and shadows bordering and sometimes ingressing the glow of the lamps it seemed to sway slightly from side to side, rhythmically, steadily. From one side to the other, back and forth, back and forth. Silently. Constantly. Its hands moved, caressing the onyx. Its frail wings beat softly, soothingly. Its squat head bobbed back and forth, its tiny mouth moving as if it was speaking, or possibly chanting. Its actions grew bolder. There came a humming as its wings beat faster and faster and faster still, until they were a grey-green blur behind its sinewy back. Its arms rose higher, its paw-like hands clapping together. The humming oscillated musically.

Slowly, with no show of haste, I told him of how the grotesque idol stood up, moving forwards across the chest of drawers towards him. And as it did so it grew larger and larger, its wings beating faster, its mouth still moving, its twinkling eyes glaring at him, glowing red from deep beneath its bulging brows.

Again perspiration coated Updike's face, his eyes staring vacantly before him in terror, whilst I gloated. Yes, gloated. Gloated at seeing him look so afraid, be so terrified by nothing more dreadful or dangerous than his own imagination. How I gloated, almost laughing out loud at every drop of sweat that fell from his face, at every uncontrollable shudder that passed through his tensely held body.

I know I should have let things rest at this, that I should have woken him then, with the memory of this, just this. But I wanted him to feel even more afraid, to feel the terror of the unknown, the unmentionable, of sepulchral horrors to the full.

Still far from satisfied, I told him of how the idol rose from the drawers, its wings spread out in constant motion behind it, its obese body swelling into greater proportions, doubling, trebling its former size. Of how its hate-filled, strangely phosphorescent eyes stared at him as its fang-filled mouth gnawed hungrily in dreadful anticipation. Of how its awesome chant became audible to him, low and deeply sonorous, with the elusive quality of vast and echoing distances. Of how its pulpy fingers grasped the bed sheets, slowly drawing them from him. Of the icy drafts that chilled his panic-stilled body. And of the way the idol, Apollyon, hovered in the air above him, slowly settling on the bed, its clawed feet biting deep into the mattress. And of how it drew even nearer, till its miasmal breath came over him and he could feel the heat from its Hell-fired flesh. Of the stench of death and necrosis. And of the feeling of horror that its darkly loathsome face inspired within him.

Abruptly, Updike began to tremble. Unlike before these shudders did not pass, but instead became even more pronounced.

"No, no!" he cried, suddenly trying to leap to his feet. Surprised, I drew back away from him. Screaming, Updike clawed ineffectually at the air before him, in between pounding his head. "No, no, go away! *Help!*" he shrieked, stumbling backwards to bump against the chair I'd strapped him to. Bewildered, filled with panic and pain from the self-inflicted blows he'd delivered to his skull, he collapsed in the chair, screaming and writhing horribly.

As he tore at the air, his body was contorted by spasms seemingly caused by agony, foam speckling his croaking mouth. I rushed to him, shaking him, slapping his face. But nothing I did could bring him out of the nightmare that had engulfed him.

The most utter feelings of despair lay upon me. What could I do? What was there that could be done now? It was as if in my insane tamperings I had discharged a stream of sheer, unadulterated horror into Updike's brain. Had I swamped his sanity, burying it beneath unclearable mounds of delusion? That what was so frightfully being enacted before me was my fault was indisputable. If not for having been stung by his taunts... if not for that 'Imp of the Perverse' that had conquered what humanity I possessed with the growlings of cant! Guilt choked me as I watched him writhe and kick on the chair, horribly agonised croakings and groans coming from his twisted mouth.

On an impulse - for which I now plainly admit I owe my life and what sanity I still have left - I ran from the room, half thoughts of phoning for a doctor flitting through my mind. But as I reached the open door a sound stabbed through my bewilderment, stopping me at once. What feelings it inspired within me I cannot describe in their entirety, of what terror and despair, of what shattered disbelief and such awful sickness verging on veritable nausea. For, before I ran, echoing throughout the whole house came an insane tittering, a mocking crescendo of demonic mirth, as I felt the cold, wet touch of a tendril reach out across my hand. For an instant it was there, but before it could enfold me I tore myself free and fled with the speed of purest panic, Updike's unspeakably ironical words shrieking through my skull: "*That's it... In the mind. Spooks have never come from anywhere else but a possessed mind. Yes, from the mind.*"

WRITER'S CRAMP

The Literary Editor of the *Digest of Horror* swung round lazily on his well-worn swivel chair as the morning's mail was brought in. Cartwright-Hughes looked askance down his long, thin, fastidious nose at the heap of battered manila envelopes that were unceremoniously dumped in front of him by the office boy. Another batch of horrors, he thought languidly, and in more ways than one, no doubt! With a quiet sigh of resignation, he picked out one of the slimmer envelopes, sliced it open down one edge with a blunt, bone-handled knife and extracted the enclosed batch of densely typed sheets of paper. His teeth should twinge every time he received one of these, he thought as he surveyed the tightly packed lines of typescript. The half dozen foolscap sheets were almost black with thick, smudgily typed letters. Lesson one for all would-be writers, he sermonised acidly, should be: always, but always type with two spaces at least between each line and just now and then, perhaps once every forty years or so, clean the keys of whatever decrepit, pre-Adamite typewriter was being used. Really he shouldn't have to read something like this. It was appalling. Even the edges of the paper were furred from wear. But, unfortunately - the Literary Editor's eternal bane! - the *Digest of Horror* was short, as usual, of publishable material and something would have to be found soon to fill the remaining eight pages in the March issue, which was due at the printers this week.

Cartwright-Hughes settled back as comfortably as his long spine would allow, propped his feet precariously on the edge of his desk and looked at the title heading of the story: *Paper Doom*. At least the title was reasonably original, he thought, pressing gamefully on. But his expectations quickly began to sink into a welter of unreadable Lovecraftian clichés - bad Lovecraftian clichés of the worst type. This was impossible! Yet, as his eyes scanned further lines, he had to concede that there was, even so, the germ, the merest germ of an idea in it. In some peculiar way the author's grasp of what he was writing about, clumsy though it may have been, did contain a dim air of authenticity. It was difficult for Cartwright-Hughes, who preferred his stories slick, to see just how this was being put over, yet it was there nevertheless.

Finally, he flung the manuscript down onto the desk, surprised at himself for having stolidly ploughed all the way through it. Normally he would not have bothered to read more than a couple of pages of any story which was obviously unusable after the first two paragraphs. Reluctantly, he had to admit that the basic plot was good, but the writing, in almost inverse proportion, was horrifically bad. He pulled out a standard rejection slip from a drawer in his desk, clipped it to the manuscript and slid it into the stamped addressed envelope which the author had wisely supplied.

There the tale would have ended had it not been for the equally disappointing input of submissions to the *Digest of Horror* contained in the rest of the morning's mail. By noon, Cartwright-Hughes was exasperated and tired. His eyes ached from deciphering the badly typed piles of manuscripts, some of which were blurred with coffee rings and other, less easily identifiable stains, which made him wonder whether some of the putative authors had had sudden, short-lived fits of good taste before sending their manuscripts to him and temporarily made more appropriate use of them for mopping up the floor.

At 12.30 Sykes, the office manager, strolled in with a list of schedules. "*Digest of Horror* is getting awfully close to its deadline, old man," he intoned portentously. He was a bald-headed Yorkshireman whose round spectacles seemed to reflect the light like spherical mirrors in a way which Cartwright-Hughes found mildly disconcerting.

Cartwright-Hughes tapped the pile of rejected manuscripts with his foot. "Literary merit seems to have escaped our hopefuls for the moment," he said, "though I suppose something might turn up in the second post."

"The Last Post will be more appropriate if it's not ready on time. This isn't the only magazine we've got to get ready for the newsstands, you know, old man, nor is it our biggest money-maker these days from all accounts, eh?" This was a rather crude reference, delivered with typical Yorkshire bluntness by Sykes, to a sharp but, in Cartwright-Hughes' opinion, temporary slump in the sales of the *Digest*. "Market fluctuations," he had said breezily when tackled about it earlier, though he had felt an undeniable twinge of concern. Cartwright-Hughes yawned. "If the worst comes to the worst I could always write something myself to fill it out."

"Just so long as it's ready for Thursday," Sykes said. "That's the deadline, the *absolute* deadline. We can't wait any later than that."

By the end of the next day Cartwright-Hughes had taken to gnawing his thumbnails. Tuesday now, there was only one more day to go in which to get the *Digest* finished. To judge from the dismal calibre of amateurish contributions he had been inundated with for the past few months he had no illusions as to what to expect in tomorrow's post. It was like that poem by Yeats, he thought:

> *"The best lack all conviction, while the worst*
> *Are full of passionate intensity."*

There was only one thing for it, he thought reluctantly as he gazed gloomily at the secretarial staff in the general office through the dusty windows of his own sanctum sanctorum, and that was to dash something off himself. It would mean having to burn some of the proverbial midnight oils unfortunately, but there did not seem to be any realistic alternative. He could, he supposed, have used an old, out-of-copyright reprint, perhaps something from Poe or Bierce, but the *Digest of Horror* was basically a magazine of contemporary fiction. The larger than normal number of old reprints over the past few months had almost certainly been the main reason for the magazine's drop in sales. The task now was to win back its readership. More reprints wouldn't do that. Far from it!

No, there was no other feasible choice. He would have to write something himself.

But what?

Cartwright-Hughes let his fertile imagination amble back over plots he had come across amongst the dirge of unprintable material submitted to the *Digest* recently. Perhaps there was something amongst these which could be quickly chiselled into some kind of presentable shape, but it was usually the hackneyed plots of the contributions that had them skittering back through the post to their authors with rejection slips tagged to their tails rather than just poor or inferior writing. Imagination and, in particular, originality were the things they mainly lacked. Yet there was one recently which he seemed to remember having been impressed with at the time, though its lamentably bad writing had earned it a well-deserved rejection slip.

Abruptly he reached across his desk for the typewriter, tugged it towards him with a triumphant grunt. *Paper Doom* had had a plot he could use, updated with a few amendments and additions. The bare bones of its plot would do nicely for the kind of filler he wanted, though he would have to change its title.

With practised ease Cartwright-Hughes' fingers tapped

out the title at the head of a clean sheet of A4 paper; *Hand-pressed*, he'd call it, in reference to the affliction the main protagonist in the story would literally have cursed upon him.

The story, which was reasonably straight forward, concerned a man's revenge against his wife's lover. Here Cartwright-Hughes diverged radically from the original story, but *Digest of Horror*'s most popular items often figured tales of gruesome, matrimonial revenge, sometimes, though not always by any means, involving the supernatural. The emphasis was strictly on horror and plenty of blood, digestible or otherwise.

The method of revenge was the only real act of plagiarism involved, although Cartwright-Hughes did not feel guilty of even this. After all, he thought defensively, the original story was unpublishable anywhere.

Sticking to the original theme of *Paper Doom*, the vengeful husband, who is depicted as having an academic knowledge of certain forbidden "Black Arts", sends an old book on demonology to the unsuspecting seducer. On opening the book, the man's attention is drawn to a short phrase on the first page which has been written in what looks like brown ink. The ink, of course, is blood. This is the key which immediately unleashes the terrible nemesis which has been sent to him. The page is not paper at all but some kind of thin, leathery substance disturbingly akin to tanned human skin. No sooner has the man read the inscription to himself than the page suddenly starts coming to "life", wrenching itself free from the binding of the book and hurling itself at the man's right hand, which completely envelopes. So tight does it cling to him that it seems more like an undersized leather glove - or as if his own hand had suddenly aged into the claw of an ancient corpse.

The repulsive skin cannot, he discovers to his horror, be removed, nor can it be seen by anyone else, as if it was only there in his own imagination. But the real horror comes when he finds, not only has his hand, in his own eyes at least, been hideously disfigured by the raddled, corpselike skin, but that whenever he is not in complete control of it his hand can unexpectedly act with an apparent will of its own - a will which it soon becomes clear is determined upon his destruction.

The culmination of the story, aimed unerringly at as gruesome a climax as possible, comes when the unfortunate seducer discovers that the only way in which he can rid himself of the curse is to turn it back on its creator. This, sticking again to the plot of *Paper Doom*, is achieved by the victim reciting backwards the original phrase which brought the page to "life" and severing his hand from his wrist with one chop of a machete. This drives the demonic skin back onto its creator, whose throat is ripped out in a ghastly welter of blood.

With the final gory paragraphs completed Cartwright-Hughes heaved the typewriter back across the desk with a sigh of contentment - a tired sigh of contentment. It was now 12.15 a.m., but at least the *Digest of Horror* could go to press complete. And Sykes would have nothing to grumble about for another month.

To Cartwright-Hughes' satisfaction there were no more hitches in the March issue of the *Digest*. Eventually, as sales figures started to come in, they even showed a slight but significant upwards climb, confirming for him his diagnosis for its recent slump. From now on, God willing, there would be no more reprints from the "mouldy oldies", as one irate reader had referred to them, but brand new, garish, matrimonial bloodbaths, of the type which the *Digest*'s readership apparently lapped up with enthusiasm - but then

Cartwright-Hughes had never had any great respect for the readership of the *Digest of Horror*. As he had once expressed it to a colleague: "Always presume that your average reader is about twelve years old, spotty, sadistic and partially illiterate, and you can't go far wrong."

Less than a week later he received a small, buff envelope in the post addressed to him by name. To his surprise he found that it was from the author of *Paper Doom*. Cartwright-Hughes read it silently to himself, his face growing pale. Finally, he jerked back in his chair and swore. "Cheeky bastard!" he exploded indignantly.

"Anything the matter, old man?" Sykes, who had been strolling past the office when Cartwright-Hughes gave vent to his outburst, poked his head through the doorway. Cartwright-Hughes waved the hand-written letter towards him angrily. "This cheeky son of a bitch is accusing me of stealing his story!"

"And did you?"

Cartwright-Hughes snorted. "The damn thing was that badly written he couldn't have given it away, never mind have it stolen. The worst I did was to use a couple of his ideas in the last issue of the *Digest*. And ideas aren't copyright, whatever this nut might think to the contrary. He should have felt flattered that I'd used them. At least when I'd finished they were readable, which is more than could be said about the gibberish he wrote." Cartwright-Hughes reached into his breast pocket for a handkerchief to wipe away the spittle from his lips.

"Write back to him then and put him in his place," Sykes said. "If you're right in what you say, he hasn't a leg to stand on."

Cartwright-Hughes grunted. He had already decided to do this anyway. As Sykes ambled down the general office, shaking his head, Cartwright-Hughes lunged for his typewriter, angry phrases smouldering through his mind. The man had almost threatened him, he thought indignantly. Threatened! He'd see who threatened who. When it came to cutting phrases, there was one thing being an amateur and quite another thing being a professional, and Cartwright-Hughes hadn't got where he was without learning a trick or two.

Cartwright-Hughes glanced at the address on the letter:

A.J. Dymchurch, Esq.,
The Laurels,
Watery Lane,
Oswaldtwistle,
Lancashire.

Well, Mr Dymchurch, Cartwright-Hughes thought harshly, we'll now see what you're made of. His fingers dived aggressively at the keys on his typewriter, venting his feelings in a machine-gun-like clatter of invective. The cheek of the man had been unbelievable. To demand - to actually demand - that he publish an apology in the next issue of the *Digest of Horror* for stealing his story! Cartwright-Hughes growled between clenched teeth. And then, adding insult to injury, to warn him of the consequences if he didn't in vague and bewildering terms like he did! Any psychiatrist, given that letter, would have had the poor fool locked up. Cartwright-Hughes' fingers quickly typed out this point, ending with an explosive exclamation mark which almost broke the key from the typewriter.

"Put this in the first post," he called out to the office boy as he meandered aimlessly past, throwing the letter, now signed, sealed and addressed, across to him. "First class post." That would show that he meant business!

To Cartwright-Hughes' satisfaction the next couple of weeks were spent peacefully on holiday. When he eventually returned to the office, happy, relaxed and sun-tanned after a much-needed break in the Austrian Alps, he found a pile of mail on his desk. "Good grief," he muttered as he disdainfully looked over the parcels of manuscripts. He pulled one out. This must contain a novel at the very least, he thought as he weighed its heavy bulk in his hands. It was hardly worth the effort of opening it since the *Digest of Horror*, as everyone should know by now, he thought, never used anything longer than a ten-thousand-word novelette. Shaking his head Cartwright-Hughes cut the parcel open to see if return postage had been enclosed. To his surprise he found that the parcel didn't contain a typescript at all but a hardbound book. "What on earth is all this about?" he wondered as he pulled it out.

Clearing the rest of the mail to one side he rested the volume on his desk. It was very old and rather ugly; its wrinkled binding looked as if damp had at one time or another take a firm grip of it and ravaged it with decay. A thick, noxious odour rose mustily from it. After touching it he carefully and fussily wiped his fingers clean on a handkerchief of the clammy feeling the book's cover had coated them with. Something about this disturbed him, but he could not figure out what... or why. Perhaps it was the smell, which was as if some small animal had crawled into the book and died.

Cartwright-Hughes flipped the book open to see if there was anything tucked away inside to indicate who had sent it. It was then, quite suddenly, that warning bells - or their mental equivalent - went off inside his head. He knew instinctively, without any shadow of a doubt, that he must not look at the page facing him, but it was already too late. His eyes were almost compulsively drawn to the dark red letters scrawled across it:

"*Mutato nomine de te fabula narratur.*"

Change the name and the tale is about you?

Cartwright-Hughes' fingers briefly touched the jagged writing to smooth the paper, which had begun to wrinkle oddly. As he did so there was a sudden ripple of motion across it and the start of a tear appeared at one end. Cartwright-Hughes jerked his hand from the book in revulsion, but the page came with it. Like a tattered, wind-blown moth the parchment flapped about his hand. It was stuck, as if glued to his fingers. Vainly he shook his hand to throw the thing from him, but the wrinkled parchment clung tenaciously to him, enfolding itself about his hand. Cartwright-Hughes knew that this was ridiculous. It was as if he had blundered into that trite story he had had so much trouble about. But stories like that never happened, not in real life! He clutched, frantically, at the page to tear it from him, but as he pulled it was like trying to rip his own skin from his hand. He cried out in pain and fell back, bewildered, against his desk, slipping to the floor where he wrestled with the thing, but it seemed to have him trapped in an iron vice moulded to the exact shape of his hand. And the vice was tightening. Crushed, his fingers were already starting to go numb. No! Noooo! He grunted with exertion, but his fingers could do nothing against the hideous, fleshy parchment that had trapped them.

For a moment Cartwright-Hughes, who was not a strong man, felt dizzy and he knew that he was falling into a faint. When he recovered moments later he saw a circle of faces staring down at him.

"Are you all right, old man?" Sykes asked as he pushed a folded jacket beneath his head. "Take it easy. Don't rush to get up."

Cartwright-Hughes breathed deeply. He had passed out, that was all, he thought. Overwork probably. A feeling of relief passed over him. It had, after all, been nothing worse than a nightmare as he lay sprawled out on the floor.

Slowly, Sykes helped him to his feet while someone fetched a chair. As he sat down, Cartwright-Hughes glanced at his hands.

"Is anything wrong?" Sykes asked; he gripped Cartwright-Hughes' shoulder to steady him, certain that he was about ready to collapse again. But Cartwright-Hughes rallied himself, though he remained silent for the moment as the full horror of it all started to sink in. He knew that there was no point in saying anything now, not now, because no one, no one but himself, would ever be able to see it. He stared in horrified silence at the wrinkled "glove" that covered his hand like a membrane of ancient skin.

When he finally felt strong enough to stand up he asked Sykes if he would drive him home. "Anything to oblige, old man," Sykes responded with the kind of over-enthusiasm people often adopt towards those they consider invalids. Subduing the irritation he would have normally reacted to this with, Cartwright-Hughes walked with him to the car park. Sykes' amiable if aimless chatter passed him unheard as he pondered on the situation he now found himself in. Every moment or so he glanced at his hand as if hoping that eventually he would find that there was nothing there and that it had all been an hallucination after all, but the wrinkled skin was there every time, and he knew, deep down, that this was no hallucination. It was real. Horribly, horribly real!

*

He thought back over the plot of *Paper Doom*. He had no doubts as to the source of the thing that had afflicted him. A.J. Dymchurch, Esq., he was the man. He was the man all right, the dirty, vindictive...! Cartwright-Hughes drew his lips back taut across his teeth in a fit of fury. Yet at the same time a grim chill of foreboding crept through him as he looked back over the story he had partially purloined. As Sykes turned the ignition in the heavy Wolseley saloon and drove them out onto the busy main road, heading towards St. Johns Wood, Cartwright-Hughes wondered whether the rest of the "curse" as depicted in Dymchurch's story would follow, in particular the determination of his disfigured hand to kill him. He stared distrustfully at it. While he was in conscious control of it he knew he was safe, but how could he possibly keep this up all the time? It was impossible, and he knew it. Yet would he have to go to the violent extreme depicted in the story to free himself of it? He shuddered nauseously at the thought. A squeamish man at the best of times when faced with reality, he found the whole idea inconceivable.

Sykes left him outside the entrance to the select block of flats in which he lived. As he hurried in, the doorman called out: "Just one letter today, sir." Thanking him, Cartwright-Hughes accepted it from him and hastened to the lift. He clutched the small, buff envelope in his left hand, having developed a sudden aversion to using the other "contaminated" hand for anything, especially this: one glance at the crabbed handwriting on the front of the envelope was enough to inform him of the identity of the sender.

Safely back in his flat, with its broad view of St. Johns Wood, Cartwright-Hughes poured himself a strong gin and tonic and put a record on the music centre, choosing a favourite Mozart concerto to help ease the tension that had gripped him and to restore at least the semblance of some kind of normality. Gripping the gin gratefully he settled back in an armchair by the window and carefully unsealed the letter.

"Dear Mr Cartwright-Hughes," it read, "You will have

by now received the book I sent to you and taken possession of the page enclosed in it. After the way in which you criminally stole the story I sent to you I doubt whether you are uncertain of what will happen next. You have been warned once already. That should have been enough. Yet I am not a heartless man. There is still time. If you carry out what I set out in my previous letter to you I can reverse what has happened. But time is short. And getting shorter. I must have your reply, in writing, soon or it will be too late. Yours, etc., A.J.D."

Cartwright-Hughes sank back despairingly in the armchair. He knew that he was faced with an insoluble problem. How could he possibly confess publicly to having stolen another writer's story? Not only would that mean his professional ruin but, even more importantly perhaps, it would make him a laughingstock from now on with everyone he knew. It was downright impossible for him to do anything like this. Impossible! He might just as well cut his own throat. There was no way in which he could expose himself like that, whatever the cost.

Abruptly, he jumped to his feet, put away the gin and strode into the study in the next room where he unlocked the writing bureau in which he kept his personal mail and laid out a clean sheet of paper. Drawing up a chair, he started to write out a reply to Dymchurch, a reply that was radically different to the one he had sent to him before. As he wrote he avoided as much as possible looking at the wrinkles and creases of dried skin that covered his hand. Instead he concentrated on trying to write something conciliatory to Dymchurch, something which would enable him to avoid the personal and professional suicide of confessing to plagiarism. Ideas floated through his mind as he wrote. An offer of money - a substantial offer of money - was one. Another was the offer of a series of stories in future issues of the *Digest*, although that was certain to send sales plummeting to a record low. Play on his vanity, he thought cynically. That was the thing. If Dymchurch could go to the extremes he had in revenge for taking a couple of ideas from his story the man must have an obsessive ego. He must have!

Cartwright-Hughes paused to trace back over what he had written. As he glanced at the letter his face became deathly pale, and a tremor started to pulse in his lower lip.

"Don't waste your time pathetically pleading. The terms have been stated. Either accept them or face the consequences. There is no other choice."

Cartwright-Hughes stared at the crabbed handwriting bewilderedly. His right hand felt even more alien to him now than before. It wasn't his at all anymore. It was possessed, stolen!

He picked up a paper knife and gently tried to prise the "skin" away, but it was no use. The thing wouldn't budge except if he cut his own skin away at the same time. Was that the solution then? Get some back-street surgeon to cut the skin, both skins, from his hand? If he did that, though, he might just as well have his hand cut off, since he doubted if so much skin could be replaced through skin grafts. He might be better off, then, having his hand amputated, properly carried out under anaesthetic by a surgeon. At least that way it would be relatively painless. Though he couldn't just go to any ordinary surgeon for a job like that. He'd more likely end up being certified by any reputable doctor. The only kind he could approach. he knew, would be someone who had been struck off, someone crooked.

Fortunately, Cartwright-Hughes had his contacts, built up over the years from his habit at one time of sniffing cocaine. Erosion of the nasal passages due to "snorting" the stuff resulted in the not unusual necessity of having to have plastic surgery performed on his nose. Since cocaine was illegal, he had had to take the prudent step of arranging through a "friend of a friend" to have the operation performed in a discrete clinic somewhere in Brixton. He remembered the anonymous-looking redbrick tenement where the squall of Reggae all but drowned the screams of untended babies in the surrounding slums. Although he didn't know the "surgeon's" name, he was told at the time by his contact that the man had once been highly placed in his field until struck off for unethical and somewhat immoral practices.

Cartwright-Hughes thumbed through his personal phone book, then dialled. Half an hour later an appointment had been made for that evening for a large sum of money. He felt sick in the pit of his stomach at what he would have to undergo, but there was no choice. He flexed his fingers. It was almost inconceivable that anything had really changed. It still felt like his own hand. It still felt under his control. But the wrinkled skin sheathing it and the alien writing on the note paper were clear enough proof that his hand had been possessed. He dared not wait for it to act unexpectedly against him, as he knew it eventually would, to bring about his death. It was like walking about with an assassin attached to the end of his arm.

When, later that day, he ordered a taxi to take him to Brixton for his appointment, Cartwright-Hughes vowed to himself that somehow, in some way he would get his revenge. However clever he might think he was, Dymchurch would not get away with this.

*

The diesel train drew up at the station, where it was instantly battered by blasts of rain. Cartwright-Hughes glimpsed a dispiritingly small, untended platform through the dirt-smeared window of the carriage door as he tugged it open. A plain sign read: *Church and Oswaldtwistle*. He shivered as he stepped down onto the platform at the cold, penetrating winds, and clutched his briefcase to him like a shield in his left hand as he hurried to the steps which brought him down to the road. He hurried along till he saw a sign for Union Road. An old man, the flat cap on his head bowed against the rain like a battering ram, was shuffling past. Cartwright-Hughes called out, asking the way to Watery Lane. The old man looked at him with glassy, red-rimmed eyes.

"That'll be up the'er," he pointed waveringly. "Tha goes past yon shops o'er there - D'yer see them? You go on past the Co-op, then a sandwich bar, *Scoffs*, then a pub, right on till tha gets to th'end - then tha turns reet. Keep on goin' after that till tha comes t'th'end. Then keep on goin' to tha left." He rambled on a few more directions which Cartwright-Hughes carefully noted.

"Thank you. Thank you very much," he said.

"Think nowt on it."

Cartwright-Hughes thought for a moment, then said: "I don't suppose you know someone up that way called Dymchurch, do you?"

The old man cocked his head to one side and looked at him shrewdly. "Albert Dymchurch?"

"It could be. I only know his initials: A.J."

"Aye, that'll be 'im. Albert Joseph Dymchurch." He spat eloquently into the gutter. "If'n I were you I'd steer clear o' that on'. Should 'a' bin locked up years ago."

"Why?"

"Why? 'Cause 'iz brains are addled, that's why. Always 'ave bin." He grinned confidentially. "If you're 'ere to certify 'im you'll no' go short o' volunteers to back up what I say. Iz that what you're 'ere for?"

Cartwright-Hughes hesitated, uncertain now whether under the circumstances he had been wise to let anyone know that he was here to see Dymchurch, especially a garrulous old man like this. There were certain to be plenty of questions asked later, and the less anyone knew about him the better.

Noticing his hesitation, the old man chuckled good-naturedly. "Don't worry yoursen, lad. I'll not press you if'n you don't want to say nothin'. I respects a man 'as'll keep a secret. Too much loose talk these days az it iz. But if'n you are 'ere to lock th'owd blighter up then you've got my blessin's lad. Aye, that you 'ave, all reet."

Following the old man's directions as the wind and rain gradually died down from being vilely unpleasant to a kind of persistent dreariness, Cartwright-Hughes came some fifteen minutes later to a narrow lane leading between a line of trees. A small, terraced cottage faced him there, its neighbours blatantly derelict. Dead ivy covered its stone walls like dried varicose veins. A musty smell of unwashed linen, cats and other domestic animals hung round the door, indication enough of how it would smell inside. There were no curtains at the windows, only discoloured newspapers held in place by crinkled strips of equally discoloured Sellotape. On the unpainted, splintered and damp-swollen door was a small plaque, "The Laurels" pretentiously painted across it in crumbling "Olde English" letters.

Cartwright-Hughes rapped officiously on the door and tried to adopt the stance appropriate to a local council official. This, he thought, would give him the best means of gaining entry into the house without rousing any undue suspicions. Browbeat the bastard first, he thought, with a load of domineering bullshit - sanitation and hygiene, appropriately enough, were obvious targets he could use. Then...!

There was a muffled creak at the door, quickly followed by another, though neither had any noticeable effect. A further creak followed, impatiently this time, and the door was suddenly tugged open. It jammed just as suddenly on the uneven flagstones inside, leaving a gap just wide enough to squeeze through. The odour of unwashed linen and animals became appreciably stronger and was joined by a further smell of cooking - this appeared to consist mainly of some kind of boiled vegetable, probably cabbage, though Cartwright-Hughes was by no means certain.

"Yes?"

An elderly, narrow-shouldered man in a threadbare cardigan peered round the doorway. His thin, angular, unshaven jaws were clamped tight, tensely, while his pale grey, rather watery eyes scrutinised Cartwright-Hughes through slightly misshapen horn-rimmed spectacles perched at an odd angle on the bridge of his nose. Tiny tufts of greyish hairs sprouted like a kind of sparse, miniaturised sedge from the tip of his nose and the lobes of his reddish ears, accentuating his definitely unkempt appearance.

"Mr Dymchurch?" Cartwright-Hughes enquired; briefcase held tight against his abdomen in bureaucratic fashion. "Mr Albert Dymchurch?" he added pedantically.

"Ye-es." Apprehensively Dymchurch glanced at the briefcase much as a downtrodden Roman citizen might have once looked upon the fasces of a Senatorial magistrate.

Despite the hatred and anger which had driven him here all the way from London, Cartwright-Hughes realised that he was now beginning to enjoy himself, yes, despite everything.

"I've been asked to see you," he said, "to check your sanitation. There have been complaints..."

Dymchurch stepped back into the house. Please come in, please come in," he said, ineffectively tugging at the door to widen the gap. "I shall 'ave to get this fixed someday," he muttered apologetically as Cartwright-Hughes squeezed through the doorway and followed him into the dim room beyond.

Confusion and dust lay about him in the living room - or whatever Dymchurch chose to term it. An old fashioned sideboard cluttered with books that looked equally old; an open coal fire from which a few sickly looking flames periodically spluttered; several armchairs, of which all but one were covered with piles of still more books; and a 1950's style bicycle propped against one wall, while above the fire place there hung a framed portrait in oils of a thin-faced man with a yellowish complexion and slightly protuberant eyes. The whole room filled Cartwright-Hughes' fastidious soul with revulsion - a revulsion born from the dreary, defeated squalor of it all. Dymchurch stood watching him, his baggy trousers and patched cardigan so in place amongst the upheaval that it almost acted as a kind of camouflage, blending him into the background. Cartwright-Hughes studied this man who had hated him so much as to do what he had done to him. He looked too ineffectual, too old, too decrepit, like a worn-out and senile schoolteacher, to have done all of that.

Dymchurch waited patiently for him to speak.

There was no point now in any further prevarication. Cartwright-Hughes, looking down on Dymchurch from an advantage of an additional six inches, said: "We've never met before, but you know me. At least, you know me enough to have tried to have me killed."

Dymchurch's eyes opened wide, apprehensive again and perhaps just a little afraid. His hands fluttered uncertainly to his lips as he spoke, carefully choosing his words. "You are, I take it, from London - not the council?"

Cartwright-Hughes admitted the obvious.

"Cartwright-Hughes is the name," he said, unclipping his briefcase. He thumped the heavy book he had been sent onto the floor. Spurts of dust erupted from beneath it, fogging the light from the windows. He reached into his briefcase again and brought out a small package wrapped in oilskins. In carrying out all of these actions he used only his left hand. His right arm was used solely to hold the briefcase pressed to his stomach. Suddenly he let the briefcase drop to the floor and held his arm towards Dymchurch, revealing the stump that terminated at his wrist. The flesh was still covered with gauze from the operation. A dark stain tinged it.

Dymchurch clucked. His eyes peered speculatively at Cartwright-Hughes. He was plainly surprised.

Cartwright-Hughes held the oilskin package to his chest and picked it open. Inside lay a wrinkled hand, his hand, his stolen hand. He threw it down at Dymchurch's feet.

"You know what will happen next," he said.

Dymchurch shrugged. "Whatever will be...," he murmured. "I can do nothing to stop you, not now." He shrugged carelessly. Cartwright-Hughes noticed for the first time a steely glint in the man's otherwise watery eyes. Was that indicative of the harder, tougher part of the man, the part that had given him the will to delve as deeply as he had into whatever realms of forbidden knowledge he had chosen to master?

Cartwright-Hughes straightened his back. "The tables are turned now, and you can learn what it is like to be cursed. And learn how careless you were to use the same curse against me as you used in your story." Cartwright-Hughes opened a slip of paper, from which he read: *"Narratur fabula te de nomine mutato!"*

Dymchurch stepped back as the wrinkled skin covering the severed hand started to move. It seemed to heave itself up from the hand, and Cartwright-Hughes could see the red perforations beneath where it had clung, leach-like, to his flesh. Like a deformed moth, the "skin" flapped itself and rose unsteadily into the air. It was then that Cartwright-Hughes began to suspect that something was wrong. For a start off Dymchurch had developed a tight, little, satisfied smile which threatened momentarily to grow. Why? But worse, he saw that the "skin" was starting to move, not towards Dymchurch, but towards himself!

Cartwright-Hughes stumbled back, falling over the arm of the chair behind him. The "skin" suddenly flapped forward. Instinctively he brought the stump of his right hand up to shield his face, but the thing wrapped itself about his wrist for the merest moment, biting into the unhealed wound, before slithering past and flapping towards his face.

"Why?" Cartwright-Hughes cried out in bewilderment. "Why?"

The "skin" slapped hard into his face. Where its abrasive underside touched his flesh it left bright red weals that trickled blood. He clutched at it with his left hand, but the perforations beneath it seemed to burn his fingers as if it was covered with thousands upon thousands of tiny, venomous, razor-sharp mouths that sucked at him. He rolled over as it tightened itself about his throat, as the room began to spin before his eyes and the air seemed to boom inside his ears. "Why? Why?" he choked out, his words all but meaningless as the "skin" tightened its grip, and blood spurted in hundreds of tiny jets out from beneath it.

Dymchurch strolled curiously over as Cartwright-Hughes collapsed, convulsively choking on the floor. His face was now purple above the livid "skin" wrapped round his throat, and small, bubbling, mewling sounds were all that escaped from his lips, drawn back agonisingly from his teeth. Dymchurch smiled as the Literary Editor's feet kicked out ineffectually, weakening quickly.

It was fortunate, Dymchurch thought, that he had not stuck to fact all the way through the story he submitted to the *Digest of Horror*, otherwise Cartwright-Hughes would never have tried, without the protection of a pentacle about him, to order a gaunt back to its inhospitable world between the planes. They became terribly, even nastily aggressive about things like that. "But you should have known," Dymchurch chided reprovingly to the shuddering remains of Cartwright-Hughes, whose swollen eyes had already started to cloud over, "that there is the world of difference between fact and fiction, and the two should never be confused. You, of all people, should have known better than that."

FISH EYE

Part One

Ray's Tale

Stood on the quayside in the village of St. Mottram, with its quaintly gabled, clapboard buildings rising up the slopes of the hillside behind him, Ray Wetherell had been gazing out across the sea for some minutes, lost in reverie, when it happened. Early autumn, the climate was mild, barely a breath of wind. Yet suddenly, for no reason, a chill, like some kind of ominous premonition, came over him. He shivered, looked skywards to see if there had been a sudden build-up of clouds, but everything looked the same. The same small clouds and cobalt sky, the same deep red sun slowly sinking towards the hills, the same gulls circling a fleet of fishing boats out across the bay.

Even when he returned to the inn, where he had a room booked for the rest of the week, Ray could not shake the feeling that something was not right. He felt disjointed, as if reality had made a subtle shift.

A couple of his fellow guests were stood at the bar when he strode in and ordered a Budweiser. Later he would have something to eat, but for now a drink would do; it might help shake the feeling that came over him by the quay.

"Hey, what've those guys got?"

Ray glanced over to where the others had gathered by one of the windows. Through the nearest he caught sight of the masts from one of the fishing boats, moored against the quay. Its crew were grouped in a tight knot on the quayside, pulling on a rope. Whatever they were trying to raise from their boat, though, looked as if it was too heavy for them to shift.

"Do you think they could do with some help?" one of the men said, a tall, athletic type with greying hair.

"Why not?" the man's shorter, darker companion said. "Are you with us?" He turned to Ray. "Might be worth our while. Might have caught some extra lobsters."

Still not feeling his normal self, Ray nevertheless shrugged. "Okay."

When they gathered behind the fishermen a few seconds later, the men had already almost succeeded in pulling whatever it was they had onto the quay. Ray craned over and was surprised to catch sight of a shell-encrusted statue almost half as big again as a man.

By the time the fishermen had lowered the figure onto the quayside a crowd had gathered. The captain of the fishing boat, a pot-bellied man with leathery skin and a grizzled beard, tried to scrape away some of the molluscs that covered it in layer upon dripping layer, obscuring its features so much it was far from clear whether the statue was of a man or a woman. One arm was raised as if in salute or some kind of command, and from the tips of the fingers Ray glimpsed the dark, coppery metal from which it had been cast, tarnished by the sea.

"How the hell did something like that get in the waters around here?" someone asked.

"Must've been dumped overboard," an old villager said. "Prob'ly contraband."

"Perhaps there was some ancient civilisation around here no one's heard about." Which raised a few raucous laughs.

"Atlantis. We've found Atlantis." The boat's captain grinned hugely.

"Yeah. And now we know what happened to them. They were wiped out by Indians," another of the locals said.

"Native Americans," someone corrected. "You're not

supposed to call 'em that nowadays."

Ray shook his head, bemused, though fascinated – and at the same time repelled – by the statue.

"Let's get Professor Collins," a large, gruff-looking crewman said. "He'll know what it is."

"He's the local celebrity," one of Ray's fellow guests told him. "Retired here from Brown University in Providence. Which tells you something when a retired university lecturer is a local big shot."

Ray edged closer to the statue, which was laid on its side like a toppled dictator. Gingerly, he stretched one hand to feel it. His fingertips tingled as they neared the statue as if they were closing in on a powerful electric current. The nearer he reached towards it the more intense it became – the more *painful* it became.

"*You okay?*"

The voice seemed to come from a vast distance away, as if he'd stumbled into a deep canyon filled with echoes.

"Are you okay?"

With an effort, Ray withdrew his hand from the statue. Immediately the pain in his fingers began to recede.

He nodded his head.

"It's strange. So weird," he managed to say.

"You're not kidding," the bearded captain said. He scratched the statue's upraised hand with the edge of a knife. Molluscs were flicked away like black poppy petals to reveal bare metal – and the webbed fingers of the statue's hand. "How's that for weird, eh?" the seaman said with an even bigger grin than he'd been beaming before, as if he could already feel the money he was certain would come his way from this find.

Someone backed a pickup truck onto the quay and the statue was manhandled onto it. Al Westmore, owner of the local garage, offered to store it till Professor Collins could be contacted. Taking him up on his suggestion, the boat's crew and several locals accompanied the truck uphill to the garage, while Ray and the others, the excitement over, returned to the inn.

"Mike Rayburn," one of Ray's fellow guests volunteered. "And this is my friend Jeb Holowitz."

They shook hands as the bartender poured fresh beers.

Mike was a six-foot, ex-football player from one of the minor leagues who coached sport at a school in Maine. Jeb, a lean, leathery, outdoor type with a Clarke Gable moustache and a pipe stuck in one corner of his mouth, owned a deli in the same town. They had been friends since High School and were here for the fishing. They had hired a local offshore fishing boat and gone out nearly every day after shark.

"And what are you here for?" Jeb asked when they settled down to their second beers.

Ray gazed at his drink for a few seconds before giving his answer. In the face of these anglers with their no-nonsense jobs and no nonsense lives, he found it difficult to admit he was recovering from a nervous breakdown after a bad divorce and the near bankruptcy of the advertising company he started up after leaving college. He had come to St. Mottram because this was where his parents had grown up. In a way it was like escaping to his ancestral roots away from the world outside, where everything he had hoped and planned for had gone horribly wrong.

In the end he gave them a brief synopsis. Brief enough to avoid self-pity – and brief enough for him not to dig up too many memories he had been hoping to forget on his holiday here.

They commiserated with him, then ordered another round of beers. The topic had been covered. Now they could move on.

For which Ray was grateful. He still felt out of key, almost as if what were happening around him was not quite real, as if it could have been a dream from which, any minute, he would awake. Talking about his recent troubles, his divorce in particular, made everything seem even more surreal. He still found it difficult to believe Janie walked out on him for someone else, that she had been planning it for over a year. That alone had displaced a substantial part of his sense of reality. Nor had he found it easy to readjust to being alone.

The next morning his head felt thick with a hangover. He showered, then shaved in the hope of helping to clear his head. Then he went downstairs to the smell of ham and eggs and hot coffee. The surest cure he knew for the aftereffects of too much alcohol.

Mike and Jeb were already there, tucking into platefuls of pancakes as if they hadn't a care in the world. They called him over to join them.

"You got anything planned for today?" Jeb asked. When Ray admitted he hadn't, Mike said: "Why not come with us? There's room on the boat. And I can guarantee you'll not be disappointed. When we went out Tuesday we caught us a couple of woppas."

Though he was not sure how good a sailor he might be, especially in a small fishing boat, their companionship seemed preferable to mooching about by himself with the threat of too many bad memories crowding in, despite the change of scenery.

"You'll need a good pair of jeans or something like that and a thick jumper. It can get a bit windy out there. Other than that we've more than enough gear for us all," Jeb told him.

It was a little after nine when they left the inn. As they approached the quay Mike recognised the captain from the fishing boat that snagged the statue the day before, and called out to him: "Have you found out what that thing is, Ed?"

Still bubbling with excitement from his catch, the man strode over as briskly as his portly form would allow, teeth flashing in the depths of his beard.

"That Brown University professor's supposed to be coming down today to take a look at it. He'll have an idea what it is, if anyone does. We managed to clear most o' them molluscs and stuff last night. And a damned peculiar-looking thing it is."

"I thought it looked a bit like the Statue of Liberty," Mike joked.

Ed gave him a wide-mouthed grin. "You wait till you see it, then tell me that again. The thing's face looks like someone's parents got a bit too friendly with a fish." His laugh was a booming bellow. "Much too friendly!" He turned to call something jocular to one of his crewmen down by the quay, when his laughter died. "Blast it," he muttered.

Ray followed his gaze. A bank of clouds had gathered across the horizon. Even as he looked it grew ominously darker. At the same time he caught a sudden drop in the temperature.

"Looks like we're heading for a storm," Mike said, the disappointment obvious in his voice.

"Yep; no fishing today, I think," Jeb added, emptying his pipe with disgust.

The clouds spread wide across the skyline, with the distant flicker of lightning.

"That friggin' statue had better be worth something," Ed grumbled, his good humour soured. "'Cause we'll get no more catches today. We're in for one hell of a storm by the looks of it."

"Perhaps we should have a look at Al's garage when

the professor comes," Mike said to his companions. "Not as much fun as going out fishin' for shark, but, hell, who knows what the guy'll have to say?"

Neither Ray nor Mike had a better suggestion, so they wandered in the general direction of the garage. Nor were they alone. A crowd had already gathered in anticipation of Collins' arrival and his expected revelations about the statue's ancestry. Ray hoped they were not going to be disappointed by the professor's expertise. He glanced seawards, surprised at how the storm clouds had grown in just a few minutes. The wind was stronger now, and he wondered how many of the crowd would linger once the storm hit.

None of them, though, had much longer to wait for the professor. Whether it was the unusual nature of the find or the fact he had nothing better to do in his retirement, it was only a few minutes before his car drew up at the garage.

There was a ripple of excitement amongst the crowd as the professor, a stern-looking man in tweeds, with a misshapen pork pie hat and a white beard, climbed out. Ed hurried up to show him into the garage.

Ray allowed himself to flow in with the rest of the crowd as the professor stared at the statue, propped upright against some oil drums. Ray was surprised how many of the molluscs encrusted to it when it was dragged from the sea had been removed to reveal the stained metal beneath. Ed had not been exaggerating about the statue's face. It did look extraordinarily fishlike. Eerily so. Ray had seen *The Creature from the Black Lagoon* on late night TV, and the statue had some vague similarities. But so much that wasn't. In fact, its face looked far more intelligent, despite its fish-like features. It also looked unmistakably evil. Its body was portlier than *The Creature*, with a pronounced paunch and a frog-like look to its legs, though its splayed feet ended in long, curved, razor-sharp claws.

Professor Collins had so far not spoken. Nor had he touched the statue, remaining a good few feet from it.

"Well, what do you think?" Ed asked eventually, impatiently tapping the scaly chest of the statue. "Is it valuable?"

The professor made a gesture as if to say don't touch it, then took a step back from the statue.

"I do not think it would be wise to handle it," he said.

"Why? Is it poisonous?"

The professor shrugged. "There may be pollutants. There very probably are."

"Pollutants? From where? There aren't any industries around here, professor. We only picked this up a mile out to sea. There've never been any pollutants there."

"You don't know how far this thing might have drifted."

"Drifted? This? It hasn't moved more than half a dozen feet for years. It's too friggin' heavy." He laughed heartily, but Ray could see he was disturbed. "D'y'ave any idea what it is? Where it might've come from? It ain't Injun, is it?"

The professor shook his head. "Whatever it is it isn't native to this area. It's made of metal – possibly copper – for a start off. And the style, the features are unlike anything seen around here."

"Where did it come from then? How'd it get here?"

Professor Collins shook his head again. "Someone may have dumped it offshore. That I can't answer. As to where it came from, it will need a more detailed examination than I can give it here to answer that. It would need carbon dating for a start off to determine its age. It may be modern. Some avant-garde artist could have created it."

"Artist, eh?" Ray could see the calculations in the

seaman's mind. "A famous artist, maybe?"

Professor Collins shrugged. "I couldn't say. Art isn't my field. But it may be."

Somehow, Ray was not convinced the professor was being as honest in what he was expressing as he was trying to make out, that he was concealing something about the statue. Why else did he look at it with so much wariness, Ray wondered, unless he also felt the strange electrical sensation he experienced the previous day?

The storm clouds had meanwhile drawn over the bay, making the inside of the garage even gloomier, and Al Westmore went to switch on more lights. The statue, looming as it did over the professor's head, looked menacing, as if it were about to bring its upraised web-fingered hands down in a savage blow. Shadows darted about its face, giving it a strange semblance of life as a gust of wind made the neon lights hung from the rafters swing back and forth.

"If you wish I'll get in touch with Brown University and see if they can examine it for you," Collins told the fisherman. "That's the best I can offer. I could phone some contacts I still have there when I get home."

Ed looked dubious at the thought of bringing others in to look at the statue, perhaps, Ray thought, because he feared the thing might slip through his fingers – along with whatever money he might make from it. But in the end the captain nodded his head. "You do whatever you think best, professor. I know you won't try and cheat me."

Thunder was peeling closer now and the first heavy rain was beginning to clatter against the tin roof above them, drowning out their voices.

"Time we went back to the inn," Mike said, "before we get ourselves drenched."

Ray decided to linger for a short while and told the others he would follow in a few minutes.

Bemused at his interest in the statue, Mike said they'd meet back at the bar, then hurried out into the rain.

As the others drifted out of the garage, Ray made his way to the professor, still staring intently at the statue.

"Did you feel it too?" Ray asked.

Professor Collins looked at him, his face pensive.

"Feel what?"

But Ray could tell: he could feel it all right. Of that he was certain.

Ray tentatively held one hand towards the statue. Three feet away, it still emanated a strange pulsating tingle that seemed to bite the flesh of his fingers straight to the bone. He drew back his hand and massaged it as he turned once more to the professor.

Collins nodded. "Not everyone seems to be sensitive to it," he said. "Ed Gamley isn't. He wouldn't have spent so much time clearing those shells from it if he were."

"Or the molluscs either," Ray said. "Not unless they like that kind of pain."

Collins smiled wryly. "Odd, isn't it?" He pursed his brow in thought. "My first thought was it was radioactive. But that wouldn't explain why most people don't appear to be affected by it. Nor is the sensation what you would expect from radioactive material."

"You can't feel radiation," Ray said.

"Quite. Which makes it even odder."

"You have any idea who created it?"

The professor paused before answering. "I didn't like to say anything in front of that crowd – most of them would think I'd gone crazy – but, yes, I recognise something about it. It's not something you would find mentioned in any standard work on history or religion. Or on cults, for that matter. I'm not even sure I believe it myself – though I know colleagues at Brown University – most of them retired some time ago now – who would talk about things similar to this."

"How long ago?" Ray asked, intrigued.

"Oh, they were talking about the eighteenth, maybe the seventeenth centuries." Professor Collins frowned. "I thought most of the tales that used to go around a bit fanciful – too fanciful to be given any kind of credence in a respected academic institution. But these were not men I would have dismissed as fanciful or naïve." The professor shook his head. "I had better return home and make my phone calls. The sooner this thing is carted off for examination at the university the happier I will be."

That night, as Ray sat with Mike and Jeb in the inn, they had news of the first death in the village. Ed Gamley, whose nets had been fouled by the statue, was found inside Al Westmore's garage, his throat ripped open.

When the three strolled out after their meal, the local sheriff and his deputies had already arrived at the crime scene. Their patrol cars, lights flashing in the gloom, were parked outside.

Sheriff Harper's investigation into Ed Gamley's murder was thorough and methodical – textbook to the letter – and discovered nothing. This was the general conclusion of most people Ray talked to the following day. Like everyone else at the inn, he was seen by the sheriff, a large, bluff, overweight man with an easy-going smile that looked a tad constrained under the circumstances. It was a casual interview in the hotel manager's office, with one of the sheriff's deputies taking notes. But Ray knew nothing that could help the investigation and had rock-solid alibis in Mike and Jeb and the barman at the inn during the time the doctor estimated Ed's death took place.

It was mystifying to everybody. Ed had been well liked in town and had no known enemies. And in a place as small as St. Mottram everyone just about knew everything there was to know about everyone else.

Adding to the mystery was the sheer savagery of Ed Gamley's wounds. There was talk it might have been a wild animal that attacked him. Allegedly the wounds on his throat could have been caused by claws or a knife slashing it again and again. It would take a thorough examination by the Medical Examiner at the County Coroner's office for a determination to be made about it.

In the meantime, rumours were rife.

Nor was the investigation helped by the weather. The storm clouds that had come in the previous day had persisted overnight and well into the morning. In the end they gave way to an almost impenetrable fog.

"Looks like we're destined not to get much shark fishing done this week," Jeb said as they settled into a light lunch at the inn, with several ongoing coffees.

The fog was so dense even driving a car through the village was perilous and most people preferred to go by foot. With its density and the lack of any motorised vehicles moving about the place, there was a peculiar hush. St. Mottram felt isolated, cut off from the outside world.

It was during the afternoon that Al Westmore was found dead in his garage just like Gamley, his face so badly torn by whoever – or whatever – killed him he was all but unrecognisable. Lying not far from the ill-omened statue on the floor of his garage, it was noticed that someone had tried to move the statue, despite its weight. It stood several feet nearer the open doors.

"I wish that professor feller'ld hurry up and get that damned thing shifted out of here," one of the locals grumbled as they gathered outside the garage while the sheriff examined the corpse inside.

Whether it was the weather or the violent deaths, but there was a superstitious dread amongst some of the locals.

Not that Ray didn't feel some of this rub off on him, adding to his feeling of dissonance. More and more the place was beginning to feel like a dream, unreal somehow, however solid everything was to the touch.

"I wonder if that professor feller's been in contact with Brown University yet," Mike said.

"Perhaps someone should ring him," Ray suggested. "I suppose the last person to have spoken to him about the statue will have been Ed Gamley. He might not even know about Gamley's death."

Mike asked someone if they knew the professor's address. It turned out he lived a couple of miles outside the village at Bluff Heights, a large house near the summit of the cliffs that overlooked the bay, built many years ago by the professor's great grandfather, General Nathan Collins, a veteran of the Civil War.

"Why don't we drive to see him?" Mike said. "The fog's bad here, but I'm sure we'll drive out of it when we gain height up the road."

Jeb said he was game. "Anythin's better than hanging about that bar all day. I don't think my liver'll stand much more of it," he joked.

Ray said he would join them. Perhaps a drive out of here would help restore his sense of normality, he thought as they headed for Mike's SUV, a huge Mercedes, several years old and showing signs of hard wear. Its engine, though, started powerfully enough and they were soon making their way through the fog out of the village.

As Mike had forecast the fog thinned out as they drove uphill, till it had gone altogether by the time they were heading along the coast road, hugging the heights. Soon they could make out the professor's house, a Victorian mansion sited as close as anyone would have dared to the edge of the cliffs. Dark wooden walls, with mullioned windows, high peaked roofs and a wrought-iron weathervane, it was probably the most impressive house in the area.

They parked on the gravel drive. Mike rang the doorbell, then waited for it to be answered. None of them had bothered to ask if the professor lived here with anyone, though the house looked too large for someone to live in alone.

It took two more rings before the door was finally answered. It was the professor who opened it, and Ray was shocked at the change in the man. His face looked swollen, giving him a jowled, almost batrachian look, while his skin had an unhealthy greyish pallor. Even his hair seemed different, thinner now, streaming from his brows in frail cottony wisps.

"We're sorry to disturb you," Ray said.

Professor Collins gazed blankly for a moment as if he failed to recognise him. His eyes were enlarged and glassy, with cold hard pupils.

"You were at the garage when I examined that statue," the old man said suddenly. "We talked."

Bothered by the roughness of the professor's voice, Ray said: "If you're unwell, we'll come back some other time."

Shaking his head, Professor Collins said: "Now will do. I feel fine. Only age bothers me, as it bothers all of us eventually."

He stepped back, leading them into the hallway. Though finely furnished, Ray was surprised to see a chair tipped over, while one of the paintings hung on the panelled walls was askew, as if someone had bumped into it and couldn't be bothered to put it straight. There was a smell in here too, a cloying, fishy kind of smell. Not of cooked fish, but raw.

"You sure you're okay?" Mike asked as they followed

the old man into what they took to be the study. There were shelves of books on the walls, a large globe of the world as it was mapped several centuries ago, and a wooden desk, hand-carved and impressive. There were books and papers scattered on the floor. An inkwell had been upended on the desk and had spilled its contents over the edge of what looked to be an expensive antiquarian book, its leather binding ruined by the ink that had soaked into it.

The room didn't look so much as if it had been ransacked or vandalised, than as if someone – presumably the professor – had fallen about it, knocking things over, in a drunken frenzy.

"What can I do for you?" the professor asked. He stroked the side of his face; his fingers looked unwashed and scaly, with large, yellowing nails.

"Folks are wondering if you've been in touch with anyone at the university about that statue yet," Mike put in. "They're getting a bit restless. On account of the murders."

"The murders?" Professor Collins' head jerked to face him. "What murders?"

"Ed Gamley and Al Westmore. You know them?"

"I know Al, yes. He repaired my car a few months ago. As for Ed, he was the fisherman who caught that statue." The professor slumped onto a chair. "Who would have killed them? Either of them? It doesn't make sense."

"Some are muttering it's because of that statue. That there's a curse on it. Though that's just stupid," Mike went on dismissively. "There's no curse in the world that'll leave a feller with his throat ripped out."

The professor stared at him for a few moments in silence, his eyes peculiarly studious in a way Ray found disconcerting.

"You been having a bit of trouble here yourself?" Jeb asked. He indicated the scattered papers and the ink spilled on top of the desk with the stem of his pipe. "Someone would think you'd been burgled, the state of things," he added.

Professor Collins shook his head. "I was searching for something – something important," he replied vaguely.

"Anything we can help you look for?" Mike said.

But the old man shook his head again, more forcibly this time.

"It will do later," he said. He gestured impatiently that he did not wish to talk about it anymore. He had things to do. "Important things," he added.

The men exchanged glances, unconvinced by what the old man was saying.

"Is Mrs Collins anywhere about?" Mike asked.

This brought an even more impatient response. "She's not here at the moment. She's staying at her sister's in Boston."

When they asked him again about the statue, he told them he had been in touch with several people at Brown University. He was merely waiting for them to get back to him as to when they could come here to look at it.

"Any idea when that might be?" Mike asked.

The professor said this was out of his hands. "When I find out I'll contact Sheriff Harper and let him know." He cocked his head, then added: "I take it no one has moved the statue from the garage?"

"Someone seems to have made an attempt," Ray told him. "Probably whoever it was killed Al Westmore. But it's there at the moment. Or was when we set out."

Professor Collins nodded, satisfied. "Very good," he muttered. "Very good."

When they left a few minutes later, none of the men was happy about what they had seen or heard at the old man's house.

"Damned strange," Jeb muttered. "He was definitely not being straight with us. There's something wrong."

But none of them could understand what.

Ray remained silent while Mike and Jeb talked together about it. He felt even more disorientated than before, with an urge to return to the old man's house. He said nothing about this to the others; neither of them would understand why he felt this way. He barely understood it himself and was puzzled why a house he had never seen before should have such a pull on him.

By the time they arrived back at St. Mottram, the sheriff had sealed up Al Westmore's garage and padlocked its doors till forensic experts could be called in to investigate it.

After parking up the SUV, Mike and Jeb returned to the inn. If anything the fog was denser than before. Too disturbed to sit at the bar, Ray made some excuses and strolled towards the quay. The waters beyond were barely visible in the fog and there was a claustrophobic silence everywhere. Even the gulls were quiet, gathered in huddles along the seawall.

Ray gazed through the fog back towards Al Westmore's garage. He couldn't see it through the fog, but he could feel it - sense it - *sense the statue inside it.* As he stared he was suddenly overcome with a feeling of dizziness and for an instant he seemed to experience a dream. It was vivid, with a violent feeling of motion, of dark figures leaping clumsily in dripping caverns strung with seaweed and huge wet boulders covered in moss, of waves crashing against the entrance, of moonlight reflected across the sea in a dazzling line that stretched to the horizon to a massive, eerie, blinding moon far larger than any he had ever seen before, menacingly low against the skyline. The glistening bodies that danced about the caverns were of the same fishlike, manlike shape as the statue, though some had odd deformities: stump-like limbs and strange, abortive tentacles that straggled from their shoulders. He felt himself try to mimic them, moving with awkward, spastic motions.

Just as suddenly as it came over him, though, the dream passed. A gull squawked in fright as he staggered towards it, before he managed to regain his balance and reached for the seawall to steady himself, gasping for breath, his feeling of unreality even stronger now. If what he had experienced had been a dream, he could not shake the feeling he had not yet woken from it. The fog that hid almost everything from him as he retraced his steps to the inn made this dreamlike quality even stronger. Even the clearer air inside did little to diminish this feeling, and he was more than ready to accept a drink from Mike as he stepped into the bar and the others greeted him.

That night Ray found his sleep more disturbed than usual, filled with hectic dreams in which movement and light seemed to clash and jar, as dim grey glistening figures cavorted about in insane dances while howling with harsh guttural voices at the sky.

"*Hiieeyyaa hiieeyyaa, aiee aiee haghanha.*"

Aching in every limb and drenched with sweat, he awoke with some of the words still on his lips. His mouth felt dry, as if he had been crying out all night, while his head ached badly, a sharp pain focussed between his eyes.

Swallowing a pain killer, Ray padded into the bathroom. It was daylight already, though the world beyond his bedroom window was still hidden behind a solid wall of fog. It was as if the world had shrunk to this small miserable patch of land. What had seemed quaint and attractive to him before, looked old and decrepit now, fouled by the cold, dank air.

Even Mike and Jeb looked concerned when he made his way downstairs into the dining room.

"You should go see a doctor," Jeb said, tapping his pipe

on the table. "You might be coming down with something bad. This fog won't make you feel any better."

Any thoughts of leaving St. Mottram, though, were dashed by news there had been more deaths in the village overnight. One of the sheriff's deputies, checking on Al Westmore's garage in the early hours of the morning during his normal rounds, had been attacked and killed. His body lay on the street outside, drenched in blood. The padlock, securing the doors of the garage, had been wrenched free and the doors were open, though nothing appeared to have been taken.

The other death was one of the crew of Ed Gamley's fishing boat. He had been attacked on his way home from a bar on Beach Street. Like the other deaths, his throat had been slashed open and his face mangled so badly that at first it was only by his clothes anyone could identify him.

To make matters worse numbers of people in the village were coming down with a virus. Its symptoms were so close to what Ray was feeling he knew he must have caught it himself. Aching limbs, a greyish, dry-skinned pallor, and restless sleep filled with morbid, violent nightmares. His eyes hurt too with a burning sensation as if they had been dosed in something acidic, though he supposed this had probably more to do with the fog.

When he went outside Ray saw some of the locals gathered by the quay. On an impulse he wandered towards them. Several turned to stare at him as he approached; their gaze was disconcertingly steady. Yet it felt all right to him. Comfortable. Even though he did not know any of them. The only thing they had in common was the pasty greyness of their faces, even more monochrome in the gloom.

Too late, as he joined their silent ranks, did he start to feel a large part of what he was begin to disappear.

Part Two

Mike's Tale

Mike had only just stepped out of the inn when Ray moved into the crowd by the quayside. His first inclination was to call out to him. But there was something about the look of the locals, pressed against the quay, that dissuaded him. There was also something about Ray – something different. For some reason Mike felt intimidated by the crowd, and he was wary about drawing attention to himself, as if he instinctively knew how dangerous this would be, that there would be something bad in their reaction to any attempt he made to attract Ray's attention. Nor was he sure how Ray would react. Not now, somehow.

He felt a movement by his side. "What's up?" Jeb asked.

"I'm not sure." Mike felt puzzled at his own reaction. "There's something odd going on. A crowd's building up and for some reason Ray's gone over to join it."

"Isn't that Professor Collins?" Jeb asked; he pointed with his pipe to a stooped figure on the fringes of the crowd. The pork pie hat from the last time he came to the village was gone and his thinning white hair was plastered about his head, but the rest of his clothes looked much the same. His arms were raised as if he was exhorting the crowd, though any words he might have been saying were muffled by the fog and the steady murmurs of the crowd itself. Though these murmurs were taking on a disconcertingly unnatural beat.

"Damn me if that isn't beginning to sound like some revivalist meeting," Jeb said, his pipe glowing as he sucked on it in concentration. "But I can't make out what they're saying."

One thing they did understand, though, was the palpable air of menace resonating from them. Affirmation of this came a few seconds later when a car pulled up by the quay near them. It was the sheriff's patrol car, its roof lights flashing. The sheriff squeezed out of one door while one of his deputies exited the other. Even at this distance Mike and Jeb could see they both held guns. No sooner had the lawmen spoken to the crowd than it surged towards them, swallowing them in a mass of bodies. There was a crack of gunfire, muted by the fog, then a terrible, drawn-out scream.

"Jesus Christ!" Mike said, a chill coming over him. He knew he should run over to see what was happening, to help the sheriff if he was in trouble, but a dreadful, debilitating feeling of fear made it impossible for him to move. He knew it was too late to help whoever had screamed. It had ended with such an awful abruptness he knew for certain whoever made it was dead.

Jeb grabbed his forearm. "I think we'd better make for the car and get out of here. Whatever's going on over there, there are too many of them for us to handle. And if they decide to come over here…"

"I'm with you," Mike grunted, ashamed of his fear. He could feel his flesh crawl as he watched the crowd move around the patrol car before some of them turned and looked their way.

"They've seen us," Jeb said. Jolted into action, the men burst into a sprint, heading for the Mercedes.

"Damn it." Mike swore, fumbling in his pockets as he ran. "I must've left the keys in the bedroom." He looked back and knew there would not be time to go inside before the mob reached 'the SUV.

Abandoning any idea of using the car, the men continued up the street. No one else was in sight. Nor were there any other sounds, just their own footsteps and the louder, deeper steps of the mob, hidden by the fog behind them. Mike looked back, saw they had outpaced the mob, then pointed down an alleyway several blocks from the inn. "We could weave our way back to the inn. If I can get inside for the keys, we can still get away in the Merc."

"A hell of a risk," Jeb told him. "Who's to say they'll leave the car unguarded."

"There's a chance they might if they think we've decided to head through the fields."

Jeb shook his head uncertainly but went along with Mike's idea. It would be easier getting somewhere safe using the SUV than trying to make it all the way on foot, especially if some of the mob took to their cars. They could cut them off on the roads out of here if they did.

Hidden by the fog from those behind them, the alleyway they chose was cluttered with crates and piles of lobster pots. They picked their way between them as carefully as they could, hoping to avoid letting their pursuers know where they had gone. Still hidden in thick swathes of fog that swirled around them, it was not long before the locals ran past the alley, continuing up the road.

"Mob mentality," Jeb muttered. "Only as bright as the dumbest amongst them." He grinned uneasily at Mike, as they set off down a gap between the buildings, one of which looked like a warehouse, towards the inn. Its walls emerged from the fog a few moments later as they approached the door to the kitchen. Beer barrels were lined up outside, alongside crates of empty bottles and sacks of refuse. Mike took hold of the door handle and gave it a push, but the door was locked. He looked back at Jeb. "We'll have to try the front and hope all of 'em have gone up the street after us."

They approached the end of the alley. It was impossible to see very far in the fog, which was even denser here near the waterfront, which encouraged them to risk breaking for the front of the inn. Again, Mike pushed the door.

"Take care," Jeb cautioned as he rushed inside.

In the short time that had elapsed since they fled up the street, some of the mob had attacked the inn. The signs of a struggle were everywhere in the overturned furniture and broken glass that cluttered the place. And, although he thought he was prepared for the worst, Mike was horrified when he saw the stocky figure of the barman, his face, chest and arms a mass of lacerations, sprawled across upturned stools and a large pool of blood at the end of the bar, a pool cue, its shaft broken, still clasped in one hand.

"What the hell's going on?" Jeb asked. "What's made them act like this? It's madness. Madness."

Mike shook his head, unable to voice what he felt. Instead he raced up the stairs to the bedrooms on the next floor. Though there was some disorder up here, too, it was less widespread. Perhaps because only the barman had been seen as a target. Had the rest of the people, the inn's owner and his wife, got away? Or had they joined the mob?

"The barman came from Chicago," Jeb said as they headed for their rooms. "He told me the other night. He's a stranger to this place. Not like the others. Most are third or fourth generation locals. Their families have lived here for decades – perhaps longer. Perhaps a hell of a sight longer."

"What are you getting at?" Mike asked as he rummaged through his stuff for car keys, then hefted a broad bladed knife he used for fishing.

"Perhaps it's only locals – locals who've lived here for generations – that have been gripped by this madness. Look at Ray. His folks were locals. And the professor: his great grandfather built the house he lives in."

Mike shook his head, uncertain. "Why should that make a difference? It doesn't make sense."

"Perhaps not." Jeb sighed. "Perhaps it doesn't to us yet

because whatever's going on here is like nothing either of us have ever been involved in before, something no one has ever been involved in before."

Mike grunted.

"If we don't get to the car soon we might not have time to think about it much longer either. It won't be long before that mob decides we've not gone up the road and head back here."

Outside it was still silent, though. If anything, the fog seemed even denser than before, so that they could barely see more than a few yards ahead of them. Wary about stumbling across any of the locals, Mike held the knife ahead of him, ready to fend off any attack, while behind him Jeb wielded the remains of the pool cue he had prised from the barman's grip.

They had not gone far when they came across a body on the cobblestones.

"Who'd they get this time?" Jeb asked as Mike knelt by the man's head, before reaching and touching his chest. He peered at his hand. It was covered in blood.

"Looks like this guy's been shot." Mike pushed the head over so he could see the face. It was Professor Collins.

"Must've been him Sheriff Harper or his deputy shot when the mob attacked them," Jeb said.

"Probably because he was their ringleader," Mike suggested, though he found it hard to believe. Yet the face he was looking at had barely a trace of the man they had seen before. His features looked debased, bestialised, his mouth wider, his open, staring, sightless eyes almost unnervingly inhuman, while his skin had a coarse bluish-grey cast like a long dead fish.

Mike let go of the man's head with disgust and wiped his fingers. They had to get to the car and drive out of this hell hole. He felt close to panic at the utter senseless insanity of what had happened this morning, at the build-up of violence and death over the past few days in this backwater village.

As they hastened towards the car they heard the footsteps and murmured mutterings of the mob that had pursued them heading downhill. Mike sprinted the last few yards and yanked the driver's door open. Inserting the keys, he started the SUV's engine with a ferocious burst of acceleration as Jeb plunged into the passenger seat beside him.

"Lock your door," Jeb shouted as they saw the first of the mob emerge from the fog.

Mike gritted his teeth as he edged forward, even now, even after all the sickening violence he had seen, reluctant to ram his way through the mob, though one part of him kept urging him to do so.

Clenched fists and thick, yellowing fingernails beat against the windows, but Mike forced himself to ignore them, just as he made himself try to ignore the panic inside him. He had no illusions what would happen if the mob forced their way into the car – and he was glad, despite the grumbling of his wife, who saw the gas-guzzling monster as a waste of their hard-earned cash, he had stubbornly held onto the SUV. Its height and bulk gave them an advantage which anything smaller would have lacked.

An iron boat hook smashed against the window beside Jeb, fracturing it into a maze of splinters.

"Put your foot down, for Christ's sake! One more blow like that and the window'll be in!" Jeb shouted.

Mike pressed down on the accelerator and the large vehicle speeded up, forcing its way through the crowd that tried to block it. For a moment it slowed when a group of locals tried to push it to one side. But the four-wheel drive was too much for them, and the Mercedes kept going with a relentless momentum that swept them aside.

Once they were free of the mob, Mike kept the car to a steady ten miles an hour. The fog was still too dense to risk going any faster. The road was narrow, with drainage ditches on either side, and too many unexpected twists and turns as it headed uphill, for him to risk any more speed. A slip could result in a broken axle at the least.

They had only been travelling a few more minutes when a beam of light appeared ahead of them, waving back and forth across the road. An amplified voice boomed out, ordering them to stop as a line of National Guardsmen emerged from the wisps of fog, automatic rifles levelled towards them.

Mike eased his foot off the accelerator and brought the SUV to a halt.

An officer appeared at his window and Mike opened his door to him.

The soldier held a cocked handgun in one fist and a megaphone in the other. "Have you just left St. Mottram?" the man asked.

It transpired Sheriff Harper's remaining deputy, Pete Volk, had been in communication with his boss from his patrol car on the edge of town when the sheriff pulled up at the quay. His radio had still been on when shots were fired and someone screamed. When he failed to get any response from his chief, Volk contacted the State Capital. The Governor had ordered out the National Guard, while Federal agents were sent to investigate the violence in St. Mottram.

The town had been sealed off with units of the National Guard, while coast guard vessels were patrolling the bay.

Lieutenant Gravowitz, the officer in charge of the guardsmen, arranged for Mike and Jeb to be deputised by Volk, who had taken over as acting sheriff. Although he looked as if he felt out of his depth with what had happened,

Pete Volk was a stolid, fair-haired man with a sombre personality who was obviously trying to cope with everything from a sense of duty. He handed Mike and Jeb rifles and told them to help him guide the guardsmen into the town. "You probably know its layout as well as me. Together we'll coordinate the guardsmen and round up those bastards and try and figure out what's going on."

"Some kind of madness," Jeb retorted, but he shook his head with incomprehension.

"Some kind of madness will do for now," Volk said. "It's the best suggestion we've had so far."

As the guardsmen headed down the road into St. Mottram there was sporadic firing as some of the villagers attempted to attack them. But it was not long before they were driven back. What numbers there were retreated into Al Westmore's garage. Mike was not surprised. Somehow he had expected it.

There was a monotonous droning from the garage as Mike, Jeb, Pete Volk and National Guardsmen closed in on it, rifles at the ready. How many villagers had joined the murderous rampage, no one yet knew. They had come across the slaughtered bodies of scores of villagers as they advanced through St. Mottram. Mike suspected most of the victims were wives or husbands who had married locals. A sick feeling told him their killers had probably been their own spouses or immediate neighbours. The strange physical decline of those villagers who had been taken over by the madness was even more disconcerting, as there seemed no reasonable explanation as to why they should have changed so much in such a short space of time; their faces had acquired a bestial appearance, coupled with a hideous coarsening of the skin and even a subtle change to their eyes, with hard, black, fish-like pupils.

Despite the armed men beside him, Mike felt

apprehensive as they closed in on the garage. It was dark inside and the villagers milled about the statue that towered above them looked threatening. Their bodies slouched as they watched the soldiers square up to them. There did not appear to be any kind of defeat in their stances. There seemed to be a build-up of aggression, instead, as if they were ready to launch themselves in a frenzied attack.

Mike tightened his finger on the trigger of his gun, made sure that the safety catch was off, and licked his lips.

The attack, when it came, was swift and brutal.

Sickened already by the torn bodies they had found on their way here, the troops cut their attackers down as soon as they moved. Again and again they fired in to them, then moved forward, beating down those they had only injured with the butts of their guns. They had been told by Lieutenant Gravowitz to take what prisoners they could once their own safety was assured, but in the heat of the moment some of the blows were deadly.

Mike nodded to Jeb. He had already recognised Ray Wetherell, even though, like the others, he had changed so much. He'd been shot in the shoulder and was slumped against a pile of tyres, his face contorted with anger and pain. Mike flinched as Ray swung his uninjured arm at him, grazing him with the talon-like nails on his fingers.

"Calm down," Mike told him, though he was unsure if Ray could still comprehend his words. "You ain't going anywhere, buddy, so you might as well give in without a fight or we'll knock you out somehow."

Jeb nodded beside him, gun butt raised. "Might be the only way to deal with this crazy bastard."

There was a moan from the surviving locals as a chain was draped around the statue. Some of the guardsmen had commandeered a pick-up and were ready to hoist the statue off the ground and onto the back of the truck.

Mike saw Ray's eyes smoulder with rage.

"Careful," he shouted back at the troops. "Perhaps we should secure this lot first before we shift that thing. Moving it has got 'em worked up."

Lieutenant Gravowitz confirmed his suggestion. "Ease up on that till we've got 'em secured." He glanced at the wounded locals. There were less than a dozen of them left alive, though there was a dangerous lunacy in their hate-filled faces that warned him that, injured or not, they were still a danger.

When the prisoners had been fastened with lengths of rope, they were herded onto the street while a group of guardsmen continued loading the statue onto the truck.

"What d'you make of that thing?" Mike asked the lieutenant.

"Looks like some kind of idol to me, though what or where it originated is anybody's guess. Ugly looking brute, isn't it?" The lieutenant grinned, his relief at having killed or captured the locals obvious.

Mike reached out and touched the statue. For a moment he felt nothing but the rough surface. It was a strange looking metal. Coppery, yet somehow there was something different about it, swirls of dim colours that looked as if they were just beneath the surface.

"Damnedest thing," he muttered, sure he could feel a faint tingling in the tips of his fingers.

When the troops had taken their prisoners and the statue away, Mike and Jeb headed back up the road to the SUV. The fog was thinning and the day was beginning to heat up as they walked. When they reached the Mercedes, Jeb said: "What do you think about taking a look at the professor's house? Out of curiosity?"

"Only if the place hasn't been cordoned off by the sheriff."

"Naw, Pete Volk'll be too busy helping to process those prisoners with the National Guard to be bothered about that place yet."

A few minutes later they were parked on the gravel drive at Bluff Heights. The house looked deserted, its front door open, leaves blowing into the hallway. The upended chair was still there, as was the picture, hung at an angle on the wall where it had been bumped. There was also the same clammy smell of raw fish.

Still feeling unsure about trespassing, even though he knew the professor was dead, Mike paused in the hallway.

"The smell's got worse."

Jeb wrinkled his nose. "There's something added to it. Something rank."

Still holding their rifles, they glanced into the study, which looked much as it had before, except that a large, age-darkened manuscript lay across the desk, covering most of the dried-up ink that had been spilled earlier. Mike picked the manuscript up and scanned the lines of closely written letters, most of it so old fashioned in style he could barely decipher it.

"Is this a transcript?" Jeb asked, indicating a newer sheet of A4-sized paper. They compared the opening lines, which appeared to be the same.

"Much unrest in the township today," Mike read. "The Reverend Phillips accused many of falling into the grievous error of Devil worship when it was discovered that Martha Craik had erected up a statue, which had been brought here by her husband from his last South Sea voyage. She had had it placed in a barn that lies on their land and had secretly had the inside of the barn made into the likeness of a temple. The Reverend Phillips announced the ill-featured statue was of a heathen idol, a Devil worshipped by ignorant and illiterate islanders, who had attacked the captain's ship and been cut down and killed by his crew in revenge. The Reverend Phillips stated the Captain and his wife had, through their unhealthy close contact with this wicked object, succumbed to the worship of this vile thing. Much was said of the Captain's illness and the strange and sinister changes which all have observed in him since he returned with it. So grievous were these changes that it has been noted he had stayed indoors these last three months. Some spoke of him staring at them, before he avoided public places, with eyes like those of a fish."

Mike turned to his friend. "There's a break in the transcript, then it picks up again some days later: The army restored order after the Reverend Phillips and Councilman Able Cartwright rode overnight for help from Bridgetown when rioting broke out in the town. Many casualties, including violent deaths, were reported. Captain Craik was captured and taken to Bridgetown for trial. His wife, Martha, was killed by musket fire, though not before she attacked the soldiers and inflicted death on one of them, he not expecting such wicked violence from a woman of her years. Under orders from the Reverend Phillips, the hideous idol was despatched to a brig and taken out to sea, where it was disposed of in its watery depths." After a pause, Mike went on: "There's a postscript, which I think the professor wrote himself: St. Mottram has been noted over the years as a place of high incidence of *premature* senility amongst its residents, including some as young as thirty, particularly amongst those who have rarely, if ever, left the village for prolonged periods of time. The peculiar form of Alzheimer's found here (if it is indeed Alzheimer's at all, which I personally doubt!) tends to be of a form that makes the subject prone to outbreaks of extreme violence, accompanied by a morbid physical deterioration in the subject's body, as if there was a malign influence at work on them. I suspect that *closer* contact with the *source* of this 'ailment' would bring about these mental and physical changes much more quickly. Is this what we are experiencing here, even as I write, now that the cause of these symptoms has been brought into the village itself? Are we becoming victims of it?"

"That's nuts," Jeb retorted, when he'd finished reading it. "The old man was going off his head when he was writing this stuff. Look at this here, where he speculates about the extra-terrestrial origin of the statue, of the *unknown* metal it is supposed to be made of. He calls it a *conduit* for outside influences – whatever that's supposed to be! It's nuts."

Mike agreed, folding the papers and stuffing them inside his jacket. "Let's take a look at the rest of this place while we're here."

They did not go far. In the living room, that also led off from the hallway, they found the source of the newer smell: the battered and torn body of an elderly woman, laid face down in a pool of blood, dried now. Like all the others murdered in this area she looked as if she had been mauled by a wild animal, though they knew better now.

"Mrs Collins?" Jeb speculated, still not used to the sight of such violence. "Do you think the old man did this before going to St. Mottram?"

Sickened at what they had found, they returned to the car and drove into Bridgetown to report it to Pete Volk at the sheriff's office.

Volk looked dazed by it all. Adding to his problems was the growing lobby of pressmen and TV camera crews milling about outside.

"What have you done with the statue?" Mike asked, after returning the rifles they'd been issued with.

Volk nodded across the road to the Town Hall. "It's stored in there for the time being. There're supposed to be some eggheads from Brown University coming in the next few days to look at it. Though whether what they can tell me about that thing would go any way towards explaining what happened in St. Mottram, Lord knows."

Mike handed him the papers they had found in the professor's house.

"I don't suppose these'll be much help either," he said.

Volk shrugged, non-committed. "I'll leave that for the experts. There's a whole bunch of Federal agents coming here. They'll need to interview you, so you'll have to stay here overnight. I suggest you book in the hotel down the street. It's plain, but decent."

That night, as Mike slept fitfully in his hotel bedroom, the nightmares began.

As fog swept along the streets.

BOAT TRIP

It had been a long day and Barry was glad it was almost over. Not much more to do now that everything had been stowed away. He gazed once more along the quay, too tired to move straight away. Rain was coming in and already he could see the first drops darkening the pale flagstones that led up to the road. There'd been storm warnings on the radio and Barry doubted anyone would go out to sea tomorrow. Which meant another lost day. Yet another on top of far too many recently. Not that catches had been worth the effort when they had gone out. They'd been lousy all summer and he had begun to worry how much longer they could go on before enough was enough. He'd spent twenty years of his working life in Pennerin Bay, but it didn't look as if he would spend many more.

"You goin' for a pint afore home?" His partner, Eddie Norbreck, cast him an enquiring glance, full of hope. Short, stocky, with tussled ginger hair and the makings of a beard, Eddie liked nothing better than to grouse for hours over pints of bitter in the Cross Keys. Five years divorced, this was his version of home life now, though Barry knew his own wife, Cathy, would be better pleased to see him home rather than stinking of beer in a few hours' time.

Still, a couple of pints wouldn't do any harm, Barry thought, too tempted to say no. Besides, after today's catch, he felt like a drink. He'd worked bloody hard, little though it had earned him.

"Why not," he said.

Barry threw his jacket over his shoulder and followed Eddie towards the road, when a black BMW raced downhill towards them. Perhaps only now seeing the quay ahead of it and the grey expanse of the sea beyond like a huge slab of slate, its driver slammed on its brakes.

"Bloody fool." Eddie spat into the road after it as the car screeched past the quay, pulling up only yards from where the road ended at a low concrete wall.

Barry narrowed his eyes. Two men excited the car. One, the passenger, wore a dark leather jacket, long and baggy, with pockets that bulged on either side. He carried a large canvas bag in one hand. The driver was slimmer and at least ten years younger, perhaps in his late twenties. He wore a dark cagoule, its hood on his shoulders. His face was covered in acne and was unhealthy thin, unlike his passenger, who was broad, chunky, with black stubble on his heavy jaws.

Low life city dwellers was Barry's immediate impression of them.

"Any of these boats ready to go out to sea?" the older man said, jerking his head at the line of boats moored along the quay.

"They're finished for the day, mate," Eddie said. "In any case, we don't do tourist trips."

"How about you?" The man turned hard, calculating eyes on Barry.

"As my friend said, we're done for the day."

Barry had a bad feeling about the man. He looked capable of violence – of hard, relentless, unremittingly vicious violence. The kind he'd only ever seen in films. Which is where he preferred to keep it.

"We need a boat," the man said.

"Why's that?" Eddie sounded unimpressed. Don't push him, Barry thought, knowing Eddie's querulous sense of humour. This was the wrong kind of man to use it on. For all both he and Eddie were strong men, used to hard manual labour, neither of them was a fighter – not the way he felt sure these men were.

The stranger turned his attention on Eddie, appraisingly. It was not a good appraisal. Barry saw his friend's face grow pale, as if he were aware that things could develop bad between them. And fast.

"How much would it cost to get either of you two fisher boys to change your minds?"

There was a calculating insult in the man's words, goading them. But the barb was baited with what they needed more than anything else these days, cash starved for months. Eddie might not have a family to feed, but he had rent to pay on his cottage and an overdraft at the bank as big as some mortgages.

"The weather's changing," Barry said. "There'll be a storm in an hour."

The stranger glanced at their boats.

"You telling me they couldn't ride out a bit of a storm? What are you, fair weather fishermen or what?"

His companion chuckled. Barry bridled at the taunt. Eddie flushed.

"And what do you know about it? You'd probably start puking your guts out as soon as we left harbour."

"You think so?" The stranger laughed. "There's one way of finding out, isn't there? Take us out and we'll see who's puking first."

Sensing it was time to calm things down before Eddie went too far, Barry said, "Why do you want to go out now? It'll be too rough for fishing."

"Do we look like a pair of fishermen?" the younger of the two men said. He had a thin, whiny kind of voice, cusped with venom.

Barry shook his head.

"Just wondering why you want to go out now." He glanced at the canvas bag in the larger man's hand, trying not to make it obvious. The bag was heavy, bulging at the sides. It had probably been a struggle to zip it shut.

"Would a thousand stop you wondering?"

"For one boat trip?" Eddie said. Barry saw his friend's attitude change. Cogs were turning in his head. It couldn't have been more obvious.

"That's a lot," Barry said. "What kind of trip are you talking about?"

The man nodded to the horizon. "France."

Barry felt a knot twist inside his stomach.

"Perhaps two," the man said. "Compensation for the weather?"

"Two grand?"

"That would be one each," the man added.

"And if we get caught?" Barry said.

"Doing what? We've passports, haven't we?" He turned to the younger man, who smirked.

"We've passports all right. All above board. Nothing dodgy."

"I don't suppose you'll want dropping off at the customs house, though."

The man smiled at him, thinly. "Not if we can help it, mate, no. If we wanted to do that we'd catch the ferry, wouldn't we? And a damn sight cheaper too."

Eddie and Barry exchanged glances, both uncertain, both of them knowing how much they could do with money like that, but neither of them sure about the risks they'd be taking. It wasn't the men who wanted to hire them they were worried about; it was the cost of being caught by the coastguard. Although it was okay to travel between most member states in the EU without passing through customs, the UK had never signed that agreement. Schengen did not apply here. Going through passport control was obligatory. And woe betides anyone who tried to get round it, especially men in their trade. They wouldn't be just risking fines or even imprisonment. They were risking their licences too.

"Cash?" Eddie asked, licking his lips in anticipation. He turned to Barry. "How are we going to get through times like this without something extra?"

The stranger nodded. "Your friend's right. Cash is king, especially when you need it."

"Up front," Barry said.

"No problem. If we set off now."

"As soon as I've phoned my wife."

"Don't tell her where you're going. The fewer who know the better, especially if you're using your mobile."

Barry said he understood, though he felt uncertain when he took out his phone.

"I need the money," Eddie said to him urgently, *sotto voce*. "If I don't get something soon I might lose my car. Not to mention the rent on my house."

"I didn't realise things were as bad as that."

Eddie shrugged. "I like a drink or two, you know. You can't have it both ways, not the way things are these days."

Barry nodded. He could do with a thousand too.

"Okay, Eddie. I just hope we don't regret it."

"Regret what? The business is going down the pan already. Let them take our licenses. By the end of the year we'll be out of business anyway."

The sky was even darker by the time they cast off. Eddie was on deck, making sure that everything was battened down while Barry was in the wheelhouse. Their guests were in the cramped space of the galley, hopefully chugging up their guts as the small vessel shuddered its way through increasingly bigger waves. The wind was rising, and Barry knew they would need every ounce of power they could get from the engines to stop the boat from being swamped.

As soon as Eddie had finished on deck, Barry asked him to take over the steering wheel while he went below to see how their passengers were doing, to find they were both wretchedly seasick. It was probably the first time either of them had been to sea - and in weather as near to a baptism by fire as you could get. For Barry it was a relief to find their inclination to intimidate diminished, though that didn't stop either of them from cursing the weather or Barry's inability to prevent the boat from pitching as violently as it was.

Barry glanced at the canvas bag, stashed on the floor between their feet. Another lurch, heavier than most, sent the younger man staggering towards the sink where he dry heaved into its stainless-steel basin, knuckles white as he clenched onto it.

"Do you still think you can get us there?" The older man gritted his teeth between words.

"It will take a while, but we can ride this out. We've sailed through worse."

"Worse?" The younger man winced, white faced and grim as he carefully clung to the galley's units till he reached his seat. "Are you fuckin' jokin'?"

"I don't think our sailor friend is joking, Toby."

Somehow it disturbed Barry the man had spoken his friend's name for the first time – if, that was, they were really friends. Colleagues, perhaps?

The older man held out his hand. "The name's Frank." He grinned before another bout of seasickness made him tense. "I don't think we need to go into surnames, though,"

For which Barry felt an inexplicable sense of relief.

"Barry. My mate's Eddie."

"Eddie with the big fuckin' mouth," Toby said. "It'll get him into bother one day."

"Believe me; it already has, more than once." Barry tried to inject some humour into his words, but his mouth felt dry. "Anyway, you'll be glad to hear the forecast is for the storm to die in the next hour so it shouldn't be long before we reach France."

When he returned to the wheelhouse, Eddie said, "How are our wiseguys? Suffering, I hope?"

"You watch too many movies."

"They're not wiseguys?"

Barry shrugged. "One's called Toby. The other calls himself Frank."

"Wiseguys with names. I don't know whether to feel better or not."

"I feel better I don't know any more about them."

"You and me both." Eddie stared at the endlessly surging black waves that rose and fell in front of them, caught for split seconds in the boat's powerful lamps.

Halfway through the night the weather eased off enough that Frank was able to climb up to the wheelhouse. He still looked queasy, but he had recovered enough to be arrogant again.

He handed Barry some coordinates on a scrap of paper.

"That's our destination."

Barry went to his charts. He looked up, puzzled.

"This can't be right. It's more than twenty miles from the French coast."

"That's right."

"Why would you want to go there? It doesn't make sense."

"I have my reasons."

"Two thousand quid's worth of reasons?"

"This time," Frank turned to stare at the front of the boat, "this time it'll be more than worth it."

Oddly, the sombre tone of the man's voice disturbed Barry far more than the words themselves. He no longer sounded like the kind of man he had taken him for. Who was he and why did he want to be taken to an apparently random spot miles from the French coast?

It was nearly dawn by the time they reached their destination. Barry had slowed the boat to a standstill, ready to drop anchor when Frank and Toby came on deck. Frank had the canvas bag with him. Barry was still wondering what was inside the bag, when the silhouetted head and shoulders of what he at first took to be a scuba diver, emerging from the sea, climbed onto the prow. Even in the gloom of predawn, though, Barry quickly realised that whatever it was, it wasn't wearing a diving mask or any sort of breathing apparatus, that its face wasn't even vaguely human, with broad, flattened, fish-like eyes and a lipless mouth crammed with rows of serrated teeth; it was grotesque, disgusting, a living nightmare.

Eddie gave a cry of alarm before clambering back towards the wheelhouse. Simultaneously, Frank dropped the canvas bag as he and Toby reached inside their jackets. Seconds later they were clenching handguns. Firing at the creature's head, the impact of the bullets flung it back into the sea; over so quickly it was as if the creature had never been there. Other than for the look of horror on Eddie's face and the guns still clenched in the men's fists, Barry might have doubted what he'd seen.

"Damn it," Toby shouted. "They're expecting us."

Frank glanced at the wheelhouse. "Get us out of here, Barry. Fast."

Too stunned to say anything, Barry automatically restarted the engines and accelerated forwards. Sunlight was rippling across the sea from the black ridge of the distant shoreline. Not for many years had Barry yearned as much to head straight for it.

Leaving Toby on deck, Frank hurried to the wheelhouse, Eddie close on his heels.

"What the fuck was that?" Eddie's voice cracked with emotion behind him. "What the fucking hell was it?"

Angry, Barry stared Frank in the eyes. "Well?" he asked. "Are you going to tell us?"

The man, looking more disreputable than ever, with several day's growth of beard and the aftereffects of seasickness, returned Barry's stare for several seconds before shrugging his shoulders. Looking away, he said, "I can't tell you everything. But you saw what tried to climb aboard, so there's no point denying what we're up against."

"Which is?"

"Something less than human. Different anyway. Though it has links to us, a common ancestry of sorts. Arguments still rage about that." The man leaned against the wheelhouse wall. "Toby and I are members of a subdivision of the Jesuits, a special unit investigating the activities of an ancient, some would say pre-human cult."

"Jesuits?"

"I am Father Francis. My colleague is Father Tobias."

Two less likely looking priests Barry could not have imagined, though the absurdity of it in some strange way seemed to add to its credibility. "What cult?"

"You won't have heard of it. It doesn't recruit openly. It is very small – for all its threat to humanity is immense. Some refer to it as the Esoteric Order of Dagon. In the nineteen twenties a branch was discovered in the United States in an isolated East Coast town. The authorities resorted to undersea bombing to destroy the base used by creatures like the one you saw this morning, while it's more human allies were arrested and held for the rest of their lives in secret camps. One of the worst aspects was that these creatures were able to interbreed with some of the inhabitants of the town. Their offspring looked human to start with, but as they grew older their other side became dominant."

"How come I've never heard of this? How could the US government get away with something like that?"

"Some secrets even human rights organisations will cooperate with if the threat can be proven to be real – which this was. Just as we have now discovered another undersea base – one we hoped to destroy today."

Barry glanced at the canvas bag, still where Father Francis had dropped it. "What's in that?"

"The less you know about it the better. All I can tell you is that if dropped overboard at the right place, it would have destroyed those creatures and their undersea nest."

Eddie muttered an obscenity. "Are you telling us you brought explosives on board without saying anything? Fuckin' bastards!"

"I've a feeling it was more than just explosives," Barry added.

Father Francis's face remained stony, betraying nothing as he
glanced at the bag. "Perhaps I had better see to stowing it somewhere safer."

Barry said nothing as the man climbed down to retrieve it before taking it into the galley.

"Do you believe all that?" Eddie asked as soon as the man was out of earshot. "If they're a pair of fuckin' priests I'm a bishop."

"Let's head back to Pennerin Bay, get shot of them, then talk about it over a pint or two later. At least we've money in our pockets for all our trouble."

"And something to feed us nightmares afterwards." Eddie grimaced. "What the hell was that thing that was climbing on board?"

"That was real," Barry said. "Whatever we think about *Brother* Francis's claims, that was all too fucking real."

Barry turned the boat to head towards Cornwall and

home. Although the sky was brightening a dense mist was beginning to seep like a huge, dark grey sack across the sea, dulling whatever sunlight filtered through. Toby – or Tobias – was still on deck, leaning over the prow. He looked tense, vigilant, gripping his pistol in one hand and the gunwale with the other. Barry saw him straighten, before taking a step back, bringing his gun up to aim at a target on the sea ahead of them. The man shouted for Brother Francis.

"Jesus Christ!" Barry shuddered when he caught sight of the heads bobbing in the sea twenty, maybe thirty yards away.

Tobias looked up from the foredeck. "Get whatever you can lay your hands on to fight them off. They'll try and board us." As soon as he'd shouted he turned and fired at the nearest of the heads. Seconds later Brother Francis was firing beside him.

Barry steered as far as he could from the heads, but the creatures instantly swam towards where the boat was heading, narrowing the gap. Eddie grabbed an iron hook, looking piratical as he brandished it. He hurried on deck to join the priests.

It was a rough, vicious, short-lived fight. In the end, though, the men had the advantage. While they were trying to haul themselves up onto the boat, the sea creatures were unable to defend themselves. Others, unable to grasp hold of anything on the boat, were swept in its wake. Those that did manage to clamber onboard were shot by the priests or hit by Eddie's hook, till it lodged so firmly into the skull of one of them Eddie had to let it go. He stepped back, exhausted, while the priests shot the few remaining boarders.

By the time it was over the deck looked like a butcher's yard. Barry gazed down at it with disgust.

Joining him in the wheelhouse, Brother Francis said,

"As they've failed to stop us it might be a good time to drop what I brought here for them. It would only take a few minutes to return to those coordinates."

Barry felt bile at the back of his throat. "Are you serious?" The only thing he wanted was get away from here as fast as he could – and forget about everything he had seen even faster.

"We need to do it," Brother Francis insisted. "We can't leave them here, getting stronger, more numerous."

"He's right," Eddie said. "I've seen them up close. They're monsters."

Barry sighed, half convinced already – against his will. "How long would we need?"

"Not much. All I need to do is drop the bag overboard and we're done."

"And get away quick before the explosive goes off?"

Brother Francis smiled. "It's not an explosive. It's a biological weapon. Something developed in the States using some of these creatures as guinea pigs."

"Nice." Barry didn't try to hide the disgust in his voice. All his life he had hated the idea of biological weapons. But these creatures weren't human, were they? Or only part human at the most?

"Before you get holier-than-thou on me you have to understand one thing about these creatures: they hate us, they'll kill us, they'd destroy every last one of us if they could. Maybe one day, when their masters return, they will."

Barry shook his head. "You've lost me. 'Maybe one day, when their masters return, they will'?"

"Just take my word for it," Brother Francis said.

So it was that fifteen minutes later they were heading back to Cornwall a widening pool of dead sea creatures floating across the sea behind them, some of which might have been taken for deformed human beings before seagulls swirled in for the feed of their lives.

As soon as they arrived in Pennerin Bay the priests returned to their car and left, adding little to what they had already said. Barry felt dissatisfied – and worried. Until now he had thought he understood the sea as much as any other fisherman. Now he realised there were things beneath its surface he could never have imagined in his worst nightmares, things he didn't want to think about, even though he could not get them out of his mind.

Over the next few days, a degree of normalcy returned to their lives till one night when they went into the Cross Keys for a pint before home the landlord came over to talk to them.

"There was a rum looking bloke in here earlier today asking about you."

"Rum looking? In what way?"

"A bloody ugly way. His face was like something you'd throw back if you caught it in a net. He'd have made a fuckin' ugly fish. He was an even uglier man." Bert laughed. There was nervousness in his laughter, and Barry realised the visitor must have unsettled him more than he cared to admit, though Bert wasn't the kind of man to be intimidated by anyone. He wouldn't have been much good as a pub landlord if he were.

"Did you tell him anything?"

"Like hell I did." Bert *humphed* disdainfully. "He wasn't just asking me, though. Someone might have told him what he wanted to know about you. If I were you I'd watch your backs. He was up to no good."

There was silence for several minutes after Bert returned to the bar as the men finished their pints.

"I might have an early night," Eddie said.

Barry agreed. He had an urge to get home too.

It was already dark when they left the pub. The town was quiet as they made their way up the road. Eddie headed off for his rented cottage, while Barry hurried on uphill to his own house. The tide was in and waves were rushing with a rustling sound though the pebbles. Though normally Barry found it reassuringly familiar, it felt sinister to him now. The sea had lost its innocence. Even while they were out on it earlier today in the broad daylight he had disliked it as he had never done before.

He opened the small wooden gate to the short path through the stretch of garden to his house. The lights were on inside and he knew Cathy would be preparing tea. Barry smiled at the thought, when he saw the large pools of water on the doorstep, though it had been dry all day.

"No," he whispered as he reached for the door handle and flung it open. The smell hit him. It was fishy, coppery and vile. Blood covered everything. At first he refused to accept what he saw, his denials coming louder as he rushed to grasp his wife's body where she lay on the floor.

Then he heard them.

Three of the creatures were stood behind him, blocking the outside door. In the light from the living room's standard lamps their faces looked ill. Strings of slime drooled from their slackly open mouths, dribbling down their scaly chests. Already their eyes were filming over as they reached out for him and Barry realised the things were dying, perhaps only seconds away from death.

The nearest of them staggered forwards. Barry stepped away from it. There was blood on its claws. Cathy's blood?

Despairing, enraged, Barry grabbed hold of a wooden chair, swinging it as hard as he could at the creature's head, so hard the chair shattered. At the same time the door into the kitchen opened behind him. He turned, too late to stop the man stood there from stabbing him in the back. His assailant's face twisted as gunfire from the outside door riddled his body.

Falling to his knees as blood – was it really *his* blood? - spread around him, Barry saw Brother Francis, gun in hand, step into the house. The priest turned his attention to the remaining creatures, shooting one, then the other in quick succession with headshots that killed them instantly.

Tobias followed him in. Ignoring the bodies, he knelt by Barry to examine his wound.

"Sorry we couldn't get here in time to stop what happened," he said.

Barry saw him pull out a stole from inside his jacket, which he carefully draped around his neck – and for the first time was convinced that the man really was a priest, just as he'd claimed.

"There's nothing more I can do," the man said as he began to carry out what Barry realised were the last rites on him. And, though not a Catholic, he found it oddly comforting as he slipped into darkness.

PRICKLY

Edgebottom Observer & Times, November 8th, 1974:

THE TATTLER -Local Views on this week's Local News.

"This week saw the burial of one of Edgebottom's most notorious eccentrics. Horace Horatio Brierley, a self-styled Satanist and writer of unreadable books on the Black Arts, was found by Police on the morning of November 1 (appropriately enough the day after Halloween), a clear victim of suicide. A disciple, allegedly, of the infamous Aleister Crowley, the 'Great Beast', whose notoriety peaked in the 1930's, Horace Brierley often figured in our pages over the past decade. Usually seen in his declining years with the small, South American ape (sic) he claimed to be his demonic familiar, he was often the centre of intense controversy, the most disturbing being undoubtedly the accusation several months ago by outraged parents that he was attempting to recruit children into what was referred to as a 'kindergarten Satanic cult'. Whatever the truth to this matter (and Police investigations were still proceeding at the time of his death) there can be few parents of young, impressionable children who will not breathe easier now that this oddly charismatic figure is no longer with us. In this pot-smoking, permissive Age of 'Flower Power', Charlie Manson... Etc... etc."

April 18th, 1975

Clouds of dust erupted into the air as the walls of the houses collapsed. Amidst the rumble of heavy stones crashing into heaps rose the mechanical whine of the crane as it slowly swung its great iron ball into the exposed innards of the house. Shafts of sunlight flashed across faded wallpaper, hung in strips from the walls and blotched with mould. There was another reverberating crash and stones, dust, plaster and paper were reduced into a growing heap of rubble.

As the crane jerked ponderously on its caterpillar treads along the terraced block of old Victorian houses, doomed to destruction to make way for a block of flats, the dust of their destruction was already bleaching the tangled weeds in their once resplendent gardens.

Within one of the few houses still intact, its inner darkness clotted with webs and the enclosed stench of decay, something began to move, clumsily at first, and weak. As a small, inverted crucifix tumbled from the shuddering wall, exposing a tiny crack, so the scratching increased in intensity - became frantic. Fetid gasses seeped into the already stagnant air, and something small and black forced itself out, blinked red eyes at the sun, its rays diffused through towering clouds of dust. It chattered in terror - or was it rage? Black lips drew back from sharp yellow teeth. Shrieked. Then it clawed its way through the tumbling heaps of rubble as the crane moved in and the house was battered into a shapeless mound behind it.

October 31st, 1978

Mrs Glasson paused for a moment as she returned home from the supermarket, heavy bags in both hands, before stepping into the shade of the entrance to the block of flats in which she lived. She listened intently. Somewhere, not far away, a child was screaming hysterically. The dingy, redbrick terraced houses opposite seemed to echo the cries with gleeful mimicry. No doubt, she thought, it was one of those rats again - those rats which the town's Hygiene Department insisted did not exist. She frowned with angry frustration, wrinkling still more her already wrinkled brows in exasperation. She could not understand how trained men, men whose job it was to hunt out vermin and destroy it, could seriously claim there were none here. Almost resignedly she trundled towards the lift, depositing her bags at her feet with a feeling of relief in her aching shoulders, and pressed for the fourteenth floor. No, she thought to herself, broodingly, she could never accept that there were no rats in this place. No matter how many times they might claim to have searched the flats and found none, she would never believe them. She wished that she could. She would have felt happier if she could. But facts were facts. And, though children might lie, cuts and scratches did not. In her opinion it was a scandal that *those men* could try to claim there were no rats in this place. If she could have had her way she would have had them fired for incompetence, though they for their part had pointed out that there was no proof as such other than the hysterical tales of the children who claimed to have been attacked by them. And some of the children, of course, while undeniably scratched and bitten by *something*, had insisted that they had not been attacked by rats at all, though neither Mrs Glasson nor anyone else had been able to accept *their* alternative. Such things just did not exist!

As the lift halted at the fourteenth floor, she glanced at the wall beside her. She pursed her lips in distaste. Another of those ridiculous drawings! Someone in an obviously childish hand had scrawled "PRICKLY" in capitals with a felt tip pen on the wall, next to an equally childish drawing of a round, monkey-like creature with spidery arms and legs and a long and very rat-like tail. Prickly! Only children, with their nasty, juvenile minds, could dredge up a name like that for a rat, or have made such a bizarre representation of a rat in their drawing. And only children, of course, would have embellished the whole thing with red about the creature's open mouth, like drops of blood.

The lift doors hissed crankily open, and Mrs Glasson

hurried out to head down the corridor towards her flat. The light seemed gloomy here - gloomier than usual - and made her glance even more intensely than she would have normally done for the least indication that any of those 'non-existent' rats might be here. At her flat she spotted another of those drawings. Someone would really have to take control of those children, she thought to herself irritably. If their parents didn't do something soon they'd degenerate into vandals. It was bad enough having rats, seen or unseen, without having 'PRICKLY' scrawled all over the place.

No sooner had she silently - if bitterly - vented her spleen than she heard a sudden patter of feet - of *paws!* she realised - racing towards her. She sucked desperately on a scream and jerked round, but the passageway was empty. No rats. No nothing. Whatever she heard scampering towards her had gone. If anything had been, of course... She felt her stomach muscles tighten involuntarily as reaction set in.

"*Prickly! Pri-ckl-y!*"

Children's voices.

Where were they?

Mrs Glasson propped her bags against the wall and hurried back to the lift, beginning to tremble. If *they* were playing tricks on her...!

"Pri-ckl-y!"

The singsong voices, though faint, were not very far away. Perhaps down the stairwell? She looked over the railing into it but could see nothing but shadows. Most of the lights inside it as usual weren't working (when did they ever? she wondered sarcastically) and what windows there were had been broken and boarded up within twelve months of the flats being built. Were they hiding down there, watching her from the gloom? Grinning at her?

"Pri-ckl-y!"

It was almost as if they were deliberately taunting her, knowing how much she detested and, yes, feared that name.

"Pri-ckl-y!"

"I know who you are," Mrs Glasson lied, calling sharply - too sharply - down the stairwell, "and if you don't stop it now, I'll go straight to see your parents!"

There was a chorus of childish giggles that amply showed their disbelief in her threat before their feet clattered noisily down the concrete steps, echoing within the empty depths of the stairwell. Their giggles, too, echoed, multiplying and dimming and becoming less human, less childlike, more... But no, they were only children, not devils, no matter how spiteful they might act at times. Mrs Glasson sighed tiredly and returned to her bags down the corridor, and her flat.

*

Although she was not normally troubled by dreams, her mind was in a turmoil that night as she lay in her narrow, solitary bed. Again and again she jerked or cried herself awake from some frightening nightmare, to spend seemingly endless minutes staring into the darkness, calming her mind before managing to get to sleep once more. The night seemed endless, like a wearying, dizzying carousel from which she glimpsed now and then while she slept things which disturbed and shocked her, things which she could barely remember on wakening, but which lingered on the edge of her consciousness, threatening to return.

Eventually she rolled over to stare into the darkness, unable to sleep anymore. Somewhere in the distance a clock tolled 3.00 a.m. Even the solemn chimes seemed weary to her ears. Weary and dispirited.

She knew that she had allowed herself to become upset too much by the childish drawings on the walls, by her fear of the rats and by the irritating catcalls of the children. But things that could so easily seem silly and be dismissed during the day, could not be looked upon now at three o'clock in the morning as quite so silly or be quite so easily dismissed, especially after a sleep that had been broken repeatedly by nightmares. Dear God, she thought, how long was it till dawn? Her eyes were beginning to sting as the minutes passed, false images like spirals of tiny red dots passing through the gloom in front of her. It was at times like these that she realised just how lonely she was - just how lonely, perhaps, she had made herself. It was fifteen years since her husband, Roland, packed up and left after the last of their increasingly fiercer, increasingly more frequent rows. A neurotic bitch, he called her, she bitterly remembered. But it was less than a week before he left town with another woman. She told herself at the time - and a thousand times since - that she had only been perceptive, not neurotic, but the word still hurt, like an unhealed bruise. She stared at the illusionary dots that milled about the darkness before her, trying to forget her memories, driving them back, burying them beneath something, *anything*, like a bad house cleaner forcing dust beneath the carpet, though the carpet bulged, betrayingly.

Slowly, as she stared into the darkness, the dots seemed to merge, drawing her attention to them. She blinked to dispel them, but they stubbornly lingered, merging still more, growing smaller but brighter. She narrowed her eyes. Were they real or not? Surely there was something there - something small and red, twin dots of light not more than an inch or so apart, reflecting the afterglow from the curtained window? What could they be? She drowsily tried to repicture the room in her mind. But nothing seemed to fit.

Suddenly the lights disappeared, reappearing again almost instantly.

With a jolt she realised that they had *blinked*.

They were eyes, small eyes, twinkling red in the darkness, staring malevolently at her.

With a scream she sat bolt upright in bed, her hand snatching at the light switch with instinctive accuracy. Something small and black seemed to dart across the room, outpacing the light. In an instant it leapt for the partially open door into the sitting room and was gone.

She jumped out of bed. Before rushing for the door, she reached for a rolled umbrella from her wardrobe, certain that the thing was a rat - one of those 'non-existent' rats, she thought to herself with a perverse feeling of satisfaction which was beginning to overcome her alarm. Let them try and claim now that the flats weren't infested by rats. Let them just try!

Carefully she pushed open her bedroom door, then strode out into the sitting room. Her free hand felt along the wall for the light switch, pressing it as she firmly closed the door behind her. It wasn't going to escape back into her bedroom. Oh, no. She'd keep it trapped in here where it couldn't escape her for long - not in a room this size.

She looked across the crumpled settee, but there was no sign of it amongst the piles of *Woman's Own* and colour supplements littered across it. Nor by the television set, with its yellowing pile of Barbara Cartland paperbacks. Slowly she stepped across the room, wishing that she had had presence enough of mind a few minutes earlier to put on a pair of shoes instead of venturing out in her bare feet. They felt unpleasantly vulnerable as she crept across the cold, hard carpet, the umbrella clenched tightly in her hand like a swollen and unwieldy truncheon. Warily she poked it into the gaps between the furniture, into a wastepaper basket full of crumpled football coupons one week old and cardboard wrappers, into the pit-like gloom behind the electric fire, its false logs lifeless. But, though she searched thoroughly, no cushion unturned, no nook unprobed, she found nothing, not even a hair. How it could have eluded her she did not know - unless, by some means, the thing had escaped from the room.

Mrs Glasson opened a bottle of Cyprus sherry from the cupboard (a lingering guest from the previous Christmas) and poured herself a glass to calm her nerves. If the rat wasn't here, she thought as she sat on the edge of the settee, her knees together, her back hunched, her cold hands starting to tremble, and there was no way in which it could have got out of the room - and she was sure about this - then she must have imagined it. She *must* have done.

She poured herself another glass as the warmth from the first began to kindle a reassuring glow within her.

As she sipped it, though, she heard a noise. It was as if someone had switched a radio on in the distance, dimmed through the intervening walls. Faint, slightly rhythmic singing, similar, she supposed, to the repetitive verses of a Revivalist hymn. She glanced at the wall clock. It was 3.05. Surely there was nothing like this on the radio at this time of the night?

Puzzled, she went to the door and unlocked it. As she peered down the corridor the sounds became clearer, resonating like a monotonous dirge. But who? And why were they making this noise at three in the morning? It was ridiculous. She would report them if she knew who they were. Some people seemed to think they could get away with anything!

Determined to get to the bottom of this, Mrs Glasson stepped back into her flat and put on a coat and a pair of shoes, the elusive rat forgotten. Buoyed up by two glasses of sweet sherry and a strong dose in indignation, she hurried down the corridor to the lift, trying to make out where the noise was coming from, though she could not imagine any of her immediate neighbours who would be likely to be responsible for it. Perhaps it came from the floor below - there were several young couples there, she remembered, her lips tightening. As she neared the lift, though, the sounds became clearer and she realised that they were being made by children. Her anger intensified. She had had enough of them already, setting her nerves on edge with their ridiculous antics, without this. That no one else seemed bothered by the din to look out of their flats - as if she alone had been singled out to endure it - only added to her anger as she approached the stairwell and peered into the shadowy darkness below.

After listening for a moment, she was sure they were down there: four, perhaps five of them. Well, let's see what their parents have to say when I find out who they are, she thought angrily. She dismissed using the lift. It would make too much noise. It would be better to make her way as quietly as she could down the stairs and surprise the little bastards. That's what she'd do. That way she would have a chance of identifying them, even if she couldn't catch them. Perhaps then she could put a stop to this foolishness for good before it got any worse. If their parents weren't prepared to exercise their responsibilities, she was sure that a severe enough complain to the right authorities would get something done about it.

As she started down the winding, concrete steps, the gloom in the stairwell seemed icily chill. Few of the wall lights were on, and the shadows that lay in between seemed unnaturally long and dismal. Except for the scrawled graffiti on the walls and the dirt and litter congealed about the steps in damp ridges and smears, it was like climbing down into a fathomless and anonymous dungeon. Again and again she noticed the word 'PRICKLY' picked out in red on the walls, alongside the grotesque drawing. As she descended the drawings became more frequent, dominating the place. There were other signs, too, like Hebrew or Arabic letters, and there were slogans, like 'PRICKLY'S DEN', 'PRICKLY RULES O.K.' and 'PRICKLY SUCKS RED BLOOD'.

She shuddered. The heat of her anger, and with it her determination, was very quickly beginning to cool as she descended deeper into the gloomy stairwell. The stairs were rarely used except when the lift was out of order and there was an unhealthy smell about them which she could almost taste. More and more she found it less easy to remember that she was in a modern block of flats, that all about her beyond the off-white concrete walls were scores of ordinary, everyday people sleeping comfortably and warm in their beds. There was a depressing atmosphere of isolation about the place which chilled her with vague but persistent impressions of vast antiquity, as if it were part of an ancient mausoleum mouldering with decay. She looked back up the stairs, but it was just as gloomy above as it was below, and neither direction seemed to offer any sanctuary. But why should she want sanctuary? she asked herself impatiently. She had only to deal with a handful of children. That was all, surely?

She hurried on, determined to get it over with as quickly as she could before her nerves finally failed her altogether. The sooner she finished, the sooner she could return to the safe familiarity of her flat. The cold bleak walls of the stairwell, with their scrawled graffiti, repelled her, especially with the morbid chanting of the children droning through the air. What could they be playing at? she wondered, unable to imagine what perverse compulsion could have drawn them here at three in the morning. It was madness.

Startling her into immobility, the chanting suddenly stopped. In the intimidating silence that followed, she automatically held her breath, her heart beats pounding disproportionately loud through her ears.

She listened to the silence with rapt intensity - it was not complete. There was a scratching noise. Faint. Light. As if tiny feet were scraping quietly on the rough surface of the steps, climbing them towards her.

It was the rat. It must be, she told herself. The children must have been playing with it - with the one they called Prickly - when they heard her coming towards them, which was why they stopped chanting. They must have released the rat up the stairs to frighten her away. Well, she was *not* going to be frightened away, either by a half-tamed rat or by whatever else the children did.

Gripping hard onto her umbrella, she raised it into the air above her head and watched for the rat to appear at the top of the next flight of steps in front of her.

There was a scuffling of feet moving on the steps behind her. Too late she realised that some of the children must have followed her quietly down the stairs. Even as she turned to face them, someone leapt onto her back. Overbalanced by the impact, she fell forwards, crying out in alarm. Desperately she tried to save herself, but the sharp, sickening stab of pain in her arm as she hit the ground made her scream in pain. She knew she must have broken it, as a grey nausea swept across her. She was going to faint.

"Can't do... can't do..." she mumbled to herself as she tried to reach out with her good arm for whoever was straddled, leach-like, to her back. From the weight and size, she knew it was a child. Small hands grabbed the hair at the back of her head, clasping it, while other hands, equally small, equally childlike, reached out for her arms and legs, pinning them to the steps. "No!" she cried, "no!" through the pain that grated her arm as they twisted it. "*NO!*" It was a dream, a nightmare. It couldn't be real. It couldn't be. *It couldn't!* More hands took hold of her hair, using it to pound her head against the steps till blood covered her eyes. Her blood!

Why were they doing this? She tried to reach out, to stop them, but too many hands were holding onto her now, and she felt too weak. Too helpless. Through swirling grey mists, that grew darker and darker, she glimpsed the children mill about her, eager young hands reaching out to grab her. Again her head was beat against the step, stunning her. "Let me go," she pleaded. "Please let me go." Too faint. Too feeble. She was going to pass out. But she mustn't, she knew that she *mustn't* pass out.

No!

She tried to force herself up, to ignore the pain in her arm. Through one eye, still not clogged with blood, she saw something being pulled up the stairs alongside her. Like a heap of old bones dressed in dusty rags, gone grey with mould. She saw a skull, thin patches of skin still sticking to it like bits of old paper, flapping where a slit seemed to gape in its throat. She tried to scream, then she saw something else, and her scream died, frozen. It was small and black, with a monkey-like body and a tiny, wizened face. Repulsively swollen like a rotten date, its tongue flicked out, licking its sharp little teeth.

Forced back onto the steps by the remorseless weight of the children piled on top of her, Mrs Glasson felt herself being dragged over. Beads of saliva dribbled from the thin, black lips of the monkey's mouth. One of the children, a boy with brown, curly hair, reached out over her. There was a knife in his fist. For a moment it wavered in the air before her face, then plunged.

November 1, 1978

"Well, Ross," Chief Inspector Innsmouth said as they stepped out of the entrance to the flats, bowing their heads against icy blasts of rain that rushed at them as they hurried to car waiting by the curb. "I can honestly say this is one place I'm glad to be leaving." He glanced back as they eased themselves into the car. The rain beat a shrill tattoo against the roof. Like an ungainly monolith, the block of flats stood stark against the sky, featureless and grim.

Detective Sergeant Ross paused to wipe his balding head with a sodden handkerchief, nodding his agreement. "It does have something about it that tastes rotten on the tongue. And as for what that old girl on the tenth floor had to say about - what was he called? - Horace Brierley?"

Innsmouth grunted. "You won't remember the old fraud, of course. He was before you transferred to this Division. Few of the locals, though, have forgotten him. Claimed to be a black magician. Third-rate Crowley. Scraped some kind of dubious living out of writing - though God knows who bought the rubbish." Despite over thirty years of service in the Force - and hard service at that, in some tough areas - he shuddered as a stray memory flickered across his mind, of the blood-splashed body on the steps. There had seemed from the first something peculiarly repulsive about the way it was sprawled. A ritualistic killing, of course. And, although there had been plenty of blood, there hadn't seemed somehow quite enough...

Snapping his mind back to Brierley, he said, brusquely: "He lived here, of course." He pointed at the towering block of flats distastefully. "His was one of the houses they pulled down to make way for it, though he was dead by then.... An odd eccentric. Had a dirty little monkey he called his 'familiar' - the kind of thing witches are supposed to have. Agents of the Devil and all that junk. Claimed to have fed it

179

from his own blood. I don't know. I only met him once, about a week before he died. Was cracking up completely by then. Said, would you believe it, that this monkey of his - this 'demon', as he called it - was becoming too strong. That it was making him do things he didn't want to do. That it was making him its slave. He wanted *our* help."

"Did you give it?" Ross asked, with a faint smile of amusement.

"What? Arrest his monkey? I told him to get out of my sight before I booked him for wasting police time. We were investigating him at the time anyway. Allegedly he'd been corrupting young children with his devilish delusions. A week later he was dead. Cut his throat."

"And the monkey?"

"Gone. Perhaps it escaped. Perhaps he killed it. I don't know. All I know is it wasn't seen again. Till now, perhaps, if we're to believe some of the tales we were told in there."

"That Prickly? The one the kids seem potty about?"

"Prickly..." Innsmouth savoured the word. "That's what made me think of Brierley. His monkey was called Prickly." He snorted in disgust. "But it was no monkey that killed Alice Glasson. Of that I'm sure. Come on." He put the car into gear. "Let's get back to some realistic police work and leave demoniacal monkeys to those who can afford to believe in them."

As the car drove off, a group of children from the flats ran out into the rain, their faces flushed as if with the excitement of success. Of a job well done. "Pri-ckl-y!" they called, running and skipping. "Pri-ckl-y!"

In the red brick archway opposite, half in shadows, an old man watched them. A dusty beard stubbled his wasted features, while a threadbare scarf was wrapped about his throat. Something moved impatiently beneath his overcoat as the children raced across the road, and he fingered the scarf around his neck, as if feeling the dried ridges of the wound which the years had hardened but could never heal. A small but powerful, hair-covered hand with hard black nails reached out from beneath his coat and tugged at his collar imperatively. He waved to the children, beckoning them over. As he shambled down the alley beneath the archway, the children bustled into the gloom behind him, an eager expectancy on their young faces which not even the cloying stench of mould could allay.

From the *Edgebottom Observer & Times*, Monday, November 3, 1978:

"Extensive damage was carried out late on Halloween by vandals, thought by police to be children, in the Moorgate Cemetery. Gravestones were overturned, and several were seriously damaged, some beyond repair. One grave was dug up and its contents stolen. Fragments of the coffin were found over a wide area. Although the size of the footprints found where the disturbances too place indicate that children were responsible, the police do not rule out the possibility that it may have been the work of a coven. Suspicions were roused that this might be the case when it was discovered that the body stolen was that of the once notorious Horace Brierley, who committed suicide in 1974 following allegations of child corruption. A self-styled Satanist and disciple of... Etc... Etc..."

Some days later

"John! Come here at once!" Elizabeth Grant took hold of her son by one arm as he strolled into their flat. "Where on earth have you been playing? You're covered in filth!" She wiped angrily at the grey-green mould that was smeared about his clothes and face, her nose wrinkling at the smell if decay. "Where have you been playing?" she said. "And don't just stand there looking at me as if butter wouldn't melt in your mouth. If you think, young man, you can go out and play wherever you please, you've another thought coming!"

The boy smiled, saying: "I've only been playing with Uncle Horace. He's been teaching us."

"You have no Uncle Horace!" she said, sighing with exasperation as she let go of his arm and pointed at the bathroom. "Go in there this instant and get washed. I want you spotlessly clean before tea." These children and their imaginary friends, she thought. First it was that Prickly creature, and now 'Uncle Horace'! Where did they get their ideas?

Unleashed, John skipped into the bathroom. "Pri-ckl-y! Pri-ckl-y!" he sang to himself underneath his breath like a compulsive nursery rhyme. "Pri-ckl-y!" And he smiled as he remembered some of what they had been taught in the musty gloom they had hidden in. He felt something move furtively in his pocket and he reached in for the small, grey 'mouse'. Its black eyes looked up at him, gleaming malevolence. Carefully he let it nestle in the palm of his hand, not flinching when its jagged teeth bit a neat little hole in his wrist and began to suck. He looked back at the closed bathroom door while it fed. Outside he could hear his mother moving things about the flat as she prepared their tea. His smile broadened, and his eyes began to twinkle with secretive glints of light.

AFTER NIGHTFALL

Elliot Wilderman never struck anyone as a person possessing that necessary instability of character which makes men, in sudden fits of despair, commit suicide. Even his landlady, Mrs Jowitt, never had even the vaguest suspicions that he would ever do anything like that. Why should she? Indeed, Wilderman was certainly not poor, he was in good health, and was amiable and well-liked in the old-fashioned village of Heron. And, in such an isolated hamlet as this, it took a singularly easy-going and pleasant type of person to be able to get on with its definitely backward, and in many cases decadent, population.

Civilisation had barely made an impression here for the past two hundred years. Elsewhere, such houses as were common here, and lived in by those not fully sunken into depraved bestiality, were thought of as slums: ancient edifices supporting overhangs, gables, high-peaked roofs, bizarrely-raised pavements three feet above the streets, and tottering chimneys that towered liked warped fingers into the eternally bleak sky.

Despite the repellent aspects of the village, Wilderman had been enthusiastic enough when he arrived early in September. Taking a previously reserved room on the third floor of the solitary inn, he soon settled down and became a familiar sight wandering about the wind-ravaged hills, which emerged from the woods in barren immensities of bracken and hardy grass; or visiting various people, asking them in his tactful and unobtrusive way about their local folklore. In no way was he disappointed and the volume he was writing on anthropology soon had an abundance of facts and information. And yet, in some strangely elusive way, he felt the shadow of dissatisfaction. It was not severe enough to worry him or even impede his creative abilities and cheerfulness, but all the same it was there. Like some imp of the perverse it nagged at him, hinting that something was wrong.

After having been here a month, his steadily growing horde of data had almost achieved saturation point, and little more was really needed. Having done far better than he had expected prior to his arrival, he decided that he could now afford to relax more, investigating the harsh but strangely attractive countryside and the curious dwellings about it - something which he had only been able to do on a few brief occasions before.

As he had heard from many of his antiquarian friends, Heron itself was a veritable store of seventeenth and early eighteenth-century buildings, with only a few from any later periods - except for the ramshackle huts, and even these were perversely fascinating. None of them exhibited any features suggesting comfort; sanitation and ventilation were blatantly disregarded and hampered to an unbelievable extent. Roughly constructed from wood veneered with mould, the murky insides infested with the humid and sickening stench of sweat, they were merely dwellings to sleep and shelter in, nothing more.

In fact, the only feature which he noticed they had in common with the other buildings was that each of them had heavy wooden doors, reinforced from outside with rusted strips of iron, barred by bolts or fastened with old Yale locks from within. Apart from the plainly obvious fact that there was nothing inside them to steal, Wilderman was puzzled at such troublesome, if not expensive, precautions against intruders.

Finally, when an opportunity presented itself, Wilderman asked Abel Wilton, a thickset man with a matted beard and cunningly suspicious eyes, and one of the degenerates inhabiting these huts, why such precautions were taken. But, despite his fairly close acquaintance with the man, for whom he had previously bought liquor and shared tobacco with for information about local legends, all the response he got was a flustered reply that they were to keep out the wild animals that "run 'n' 'ide in th' 'ills, where none but those pohzessed go; where they wait for us, coming down 'ere at night, a 'untin'," or so Wilton claimed. But his suddenly narrowed eyes and obvious dislike of the subject belied him, though Wilderman tactfully decided to accept this explanation for the moment. After all, it would do him no good, he reasoned, to go around accusing people of being liars. It could only result in drawing onto himself the animosity of Wilton's kinfolk who, ignorant though they were, were extremely susceptible to insult.

However, after having noticed this point about the clustered huts on the outskirts of Heron, Wilderman realised that all of the other houses that he had entered also had unusually sturdy locks. Not only on their doors, either; most had padlocks or bolts across the shutters on their windows, too, though they were already protected by bars on the ground floors. But, when he questioned someone about this, he again received a muttered reply about wild beasts, as well as the danger of thieves, and again he did not believe it. He could have been convinced of the possibility of thieves, even in the worthless huts, but how could he possibly accept the wild animals when he had never even seen a sign of them during his now frequent rambles across the hills? Certainly none that were of any danger at all to man. And so, realising then that any further approaches on this subject would probably only bring similar results, he did not pursue it any further, though he fully intended to keep it in mind. Perhaps, he thought, this was what had been troubling him all along.

It was at this time, in late October, when he was beginning to pay closer attention to his surroundings, that he first realised that no one ever left their houses after dusk. Even he himself had never gone out after nightfall before since it had kept light until late. But as the nights became longer, creeping remorselessly into the dwindling days, this universal peculiarity in Heron became more and more apparent to him, and adding yet another mystery to be solved.

The first time he had this brought to his attention was one evening when he tried to leave the inn and found that both the front and back doors were locked. Irritably he strode up to Mrs Jowitt, an elderly woman, grey of face and hair, with needle-like fingers and brown teeth that seemed to blend in with the gloom of the sitting-room where she sat knitting a shawl. Without preamble he asked why the inn had been locked at so early an hour.

For a moment she seemed to have been stunned into silence by his outburst and immediately stopped her work to turn towards him. In that brief instant her face had paled into a waxen mask, her eyes, like Wilton's, narrowing menacingly - or were they, Wilderman conjectured in surprise, hooded to hide the barely concealed fear he felt he could glimpse between the quivering lids?

"We always lock up at night, Mr Wilderman," she drawled at length. "Always 'ave an' always will do. It's one of our ways. P'raps it's foolish - you might think so - but that's our custom. Any'ow, there's no reason to go out when it's dark, is there? There's nowt 'ere i' the way of entertainment. Besides, can't be too careful. More goes on than you'd suspect - or want to. Not only is there animals that'd kill us in our sleep, but some o' them in the 'uts - I'm not sayin' who, mind you - wouldn't think twice o' breakin' and takin' all I've got if I didn't lock 'em out."

Her reply left little with which Wilderman could

legitimately argue, without seeming to do so solely for the sake of argument, and he was loath to antagonise her. Always he was aware that he was here only on the townspeople's toleration; they could very easily snub him or even do him physical damage and get away with it. Justice (a dubious word here) was at best rudimentary. It depended for a large part on family connections and as good as open bribery. At its worst and most frequent, it depended on personal revenge, reminding Wilderman distastefully of the outdated duelling system of latter-day Europe, though with significantly less notice taken of honour.

Convinced that fear of wild animals was not the reason for Mrs Jowitt's locking of the doors after dusk, Wilderman became determined to delve further into this aggravating mystery.

The next morning, rising deliberately at dawn, he hurried noiselessly down the staircase to find his landlady busy unlocking the front door. So engrossed was she in the seemingly arduous task that she did not notice his presence.

Finally succeeding in turning the last of the keys, she cautiously prised the door open and peered uneasily outside. Evidently seeing nothing to alarm her, she threw the door open and knelt down to pick up an enamel dish from the worn doorstep outside. Filled with curiosity, Wilderman tried to see what was on it, but could only glimpse a faint red smear that might have been a reflection of the sun rising liquescently above the hills.

Before Mrs Jowitt could turn and see him, he retraced his steps to the second floor, walking back down again loudly and calling a greeting to her. After a few brief, but necessary, comments about the weather, he left, stepping out into the cold, but refreshing early morning air. The narrow streets were still half-obscured by mists, through which beams of sunlight shone against the newly unshuttered windows like drops of molten gold.

As he slowly made his way down the winding street he could not help but notice the plates and dishes left on many of the doorsteps. Some others had been shattered and left on the stagnant gutter that ran down the centre of the street to a mud-clogged grate at the end.

It was immediately obvious to Wilderman that these dishes had contained meat - raw meat - as shown by the watery stains of blood still on them. But why should the villagers leave food out like this? he asked himself. Every one of them, including those in the fetid huts, even though they had little enough to eat at the best of times.

Such behaviour as was evident here seemed ludicrous to him. Why, indeed, should they have left food out like this, presumably for animals, when they dared not go out after nightfall for fear of those very creatures which the meat would only attract? It didn't make sense. That people in Heron were not exceptionally kind and generous to animals he knew; quite the opposite, in fact. Already he had seen what remained of one dog - a wolfhound with Alsatian blood in its savage veins - that made a nuisance of itself one Saturday on Market Street. Its mangled carcass, gory and flayed to the bone, had almost defied description after some ten or so heavy boots, backed by resentful legs, had crushed it writhing into the cobbles. Then why, if they had no other feelings but contempt for their own animals, should they be so unnaturally benevolent to dangerous and anonymous beasts?

Obviously, though, no one would tell him why they did this. Already he had tried questioning them about their heavily locked doors with only the barest of results. There was, he knew, only one way in which he would have the slightest chance of finding out anything more, and that was to see for himself what came for the food.

Preparing himself for the nocturnal vigil, he returned to his room and spent the rest of the day rereading several of his notes and continuing his treatise from where he had left off the previous day.

Nightfall soon came, and with it an all-penetrating fog that tainted everything, even the inside of his room, with an obscuring mist. Sitting on a high-backed chair by the window, he cursed it, but was adamant that the fulfilment of his malign curiosity would not be foiled by a mist.

Almost as soon as the sun had disappeared beneath the fog-hidden mountains, Wilderman heard several nearby doors being opened, though no one called out. The only sound was that of the indistinct clatter of plates being placed on the pavements, before the doors were hastily slammed shut and locked. Following this came an absolute silence in which nothing stirred on the fog-shrouded street. It was as though all life and movement had come to an end, disturbed only by the clock atop the hearth within his room, as it slowly ticked out the laboured seconds and minutes. Then something caught his attention.

Looking out over the worn windowsill, he stared down at the street, trying to penetrate the myopic mist. Some thing or things were coming down the street. But the noises were strange and disturbing, not the anticipated padded footfalls of wildcats or dogs gone feral from neglect or cruelty. No, the sounds that reached his ears were far from expected, but were like a sibilant slithering sound, as of something possessed by an iron determination dragging itself sluggishly across the cobbles.

A tin plate was noisily upended and went clattering down the street, coming to a halt at the raised pavement beneath his window. As he leaned out further to look, he saw a darkish, shadowy thing, a hulking shape, appear. For several moments following this intrusion he heard no more until the creature found its food and began to devour it.

Pulling himself together, Wilderman shouted to scare whatever was beneath him away. But as his cry echoed dismally down the street to the clock tower in the square at the end, it sounded even more hysterical at each dimming repetition, more forlorn and pathetic. There was only an instant's pause before he heard the other milling creatures on the street begin to drag themselves across and along it, deserting their food to make their way to the inn.

And with them came a fiendish tittering, ghoulish in its overtly inhuman form, devoid of all but the foulest of feelings: hatred, lust and, surprising Wilderman in his interpretation of it, an almost insatiable greed. So clear was it in the vague sounds shuddering below, that he felt the tremors of panic growing inside him, sweat streaming down his face. Again, after an inner struggle, he called out, his voice rasping with fear.

In answer came a scratching at the base of the inn beneath his window, as though something sought to surmount the decaying barrier.

More shapes were gathering on the street, slithering towards the inn and scratching at it. Trembling fiercely, he realised why the villagers took such precautions as they did, and why none spoke or left their houses at night, leaving the village as though deserted. But the facade had been broken. They knew he was here; they had heard him.

Picking up a heavy, fore-edged book, he hurled it down at the creatures below. As it struck them there was the sound as of a large stone falling into mud, and then a series of cracks like breaking bones, thin, brittle ones, shattered by the copper-bound book. At this the horrid sounds increased into a crescendo of fiendish glee. A shriek as inhuman as the others, yet still possessing the wretched qualities of agony and terror, echoed down the street. But loud and terrible though this was, no one in any of the neighbouring houses appeared to see what was happening. All shutters and doors remained closed.

A sudden breeze, that died almost as soon as it came, sent the fog floundering from the street in scattering wisps. Wilderman saw the shapes more clearly, though they were blurred even now by the gloom. For a time he had thought them to be animals, hybrids of some sort, but what he now saw was neither wholly bestial nor human, but possessed - or seemed to be possessed, in the shadow world they inhabited - of the worst features of each. Hunched, with massive backs above stunted heads that hung low upon their chests, they dragged themselves along with skeletal arms which, when outstretched above their shoulders into the diffused light from his room, proved white and leprous, crumbling as though riddled with decay. Tapering to gangrenous stumps, their fingers opened slowly, painfully, and closed again before the mist returned and resealed them in a spectral haze.

When once more half-hidden in the fog, Wilderman saw that the shadows were converging upon one spot which then became progressively clearer, more distinct. And suddenly, with the self-consuming quicklime of fear, he realised why: slowly, inevitably, they were climbing upon each other to form a hillock, a living hillock to his window!

Again, he threw a book at them, and then another and another, each more savagely than the last. But though they seemed to crash into and through the skulking bodies, the mound still continued to grow. And from the nethermost extremes of the mist-filled street, he could make out others slithering and shuffling towards the inn.

In alarm Wilderman threw himself back from the window, slamming and fastening its shutters as he did so. Then, in a fit of nausea, he staggered to a basin on his dresser and was violently sick. Outside, the tittering was continuing to grow louder, nearer. Awful in its surfeit of abhorrence, it filled Wilderman with increasingly more dread at every passing instant. With movements strained from forcing himself to resist the panic he felt growing inside him, he crept behind the writing desk in the centre of the room until, with his hands clenched tightly on it, he faced the shuttered window. His face shivering uncontrollably as his eyes stared harder and harder at the window... waiting, dreading the end of his wait, fearing the expected arrival.

And still, from outside, the gibbering, the hellish, inhuman giggling increased in volume until suddenly it ended and a scratching of claws on wood took its place. The shutters shook and rattled on their creaking hinges so violently that they threatened to give way at any moment.

And then they did.

Myriad shrieks of fiendish glee flooded Wilderman's room. Shrieks that mingled with, and then utterly overpowered and drowned, the tortured screams of anguish, terror and then agony that were human, and which ended as the slobbering, tearing sounds of eating took their place.

*

The next day, as a reluctant sun reared itself in a blood-red crescent above the pale pine forests to the east, the locked door to Wilderman's room was forced open by two of Mrs Jowitt's permanent guests after her unsuccessful attempt to rouse him earlier. As the men pushed and beat at the old oak panels, she waited behind them, shivering as she remembered the cries of the night when she lay locked in her room down the passageway, wide-eyed in fear and dread. So had, as she could tell by their red-rimmed eyes and fearful expressions, the two men.

With a mournful rending of wood, the door fell inwards. As the men were contorted with disgust and nausea, Mrs Jowitt looked into the room and screamed. Inside, the room was cluttered with shattered and overturned furniture, scratched till the wood was bare, sheets torn into shreds, and a skeletal thing that lay amidst a bloody upheaval of tattered books, manuscripts, pens and cloth, bones scattered to every corner.

*

Though the circumstances surrounding Wilderman's death did not show even the vaguest trace of suicide, this was the verdict solemnly reached by the coroner, a native of Heron, four days later in the poorly lit village hall.

All through the hastily completed inquest Wilderman's various relatives were refused permission to view his remains before they were interred in the cemetery on the outskirts of the village. The coroner said that his mode of self-destruction - drowning himself in a nearby river - and the fact that it had taken nearly a week to find him, had left the body in a state that was most definitely not wise to be seen.

"It would be better to remember him as he was," said the wrinkled old man, nervously cleaning his wire-framed bifocals, "than as he is now."

While outside, unnoticed by the visitors, the church warden completed his daily task of beating down the disrupted earth on the graves in the wild and tawny burial ground, whispering a useless prayer to himself before returning to his home for supper.

AFTER NIGHTFALL

DAVID A. RILEY

ILLUSTRATIONS

Although some of the illustrations by Jim Pitts that appear in this book are brand new, some stretch back nearly fifty years - for almost as long as we have known each other, in fact. Here is a list of what stories they relate to and where they were originally published.

THE FANTASTICAL ART
OF JIM PITTS

Two soft cover volumes of Jim Pitts' amazing artwork, *The Fantastical Art of Jim Pitts*, are available from amazon, Barnes & Noble and elsewhere.

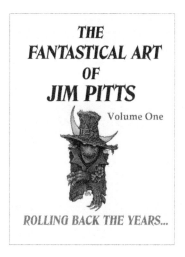

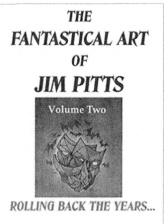

Both books are also available in one hard cover volume published as a signed, limited, and numbered edition. Copies are available direct from the publisher, price £45 plus postage and packing.

Email: *paralleluniversepublications@gmx.co.uk* for details or go to our website at Parallel Universe Publications to order online.
https://paralleluniversepublications.blogspot.com/

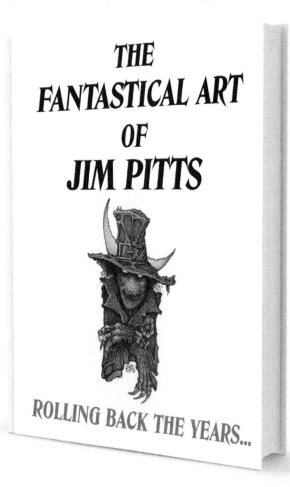

DAVID A. RILEY BOOKS

Printed in Great Britain
by Amazon